A CRACKING
OF SPINES

A CRACKING
OF SPINES

ROY HARLEY LEWIS

ST. MARTIN'S PRESS
NEW YORK

Copyright © 1981 by Roy Harley Lewis
For information, write: St. Martin's Press,
175 Fifth Avenue, New York, N.Y. 10010
Manufactured in the United States of America

Library of Congress Cataloging in Publication Data

Lewis, Roy Harley.
A cracking of spines.

I. Title.
PR6062.E9543C7   1982   823'.914   81-14526
ISBN 0-312-17073-4   AACR2

AUTHOR'S NOTE

Bibliophiles will, I hope, forgive me for the occasional liberty I have taken for the sake of convenience. The Libraries Association, for example, does have a Rare Books Group newsletter, but I have chosen to publish it monthly, not quarterly. The characters are, of course, my own and bear no resemblance to any person living or dead.

PREFACE

The thin man was conscious of his knees shaking as he clambered awkwardly and almost blindly down the trailing rope ladder from the domed skylight forty feet above the library. All the time he had to resist the overtures of panic by forcing himself to relax, clearing the mind and concentrating on one thing only—placing his feet one after the other very precisely on the swaying and elusive rungs unseen below. But the unfamiliarity of the situation made matters worse, accentuating the difficulty he had in co-ordinating his limbs.

The sense of unreality increased his nervousness. Beads of perspiration began to assemble at his eyebrows and eventually moved, ponderously at first but with increasing speed, down the bridge of his nose. The tight skin behind his ears was also drenched in sweat and he had visions of his spectacles slipping, making him frightened to look down in case they actually slid off. He even risked letting go of the ladder with his left hand to adjust them although within another second they seemed to be slipping again.

The men with him were experienced and apparently fearless but the huge library was silent and in total darkness and he was consumed with an unreasonable dread of the unknown, of the retribution that might lurk in the shadows. God, how he could do with a cigarette to steady his nerves! They had made him leave the pack behind and it had seemed reasonable at the time. Now it seemed over-cautious. His eyes moved instinctively around the long shelf-lined room and suddenly he was conscious that it was not as silent as he had imagined . . . the highly polished, worn floorboards, the towering oak bookcases, crested with weird creatures and cherubs, even the leather-bound volumes in their neat military-style formations, seemed to be breathing . . . surely that was what he could hear . . . no, it must be a trick of his imagination . . .

"For Chrissake, hurry up!" urged the hooded man below. And as though on cue the second man above him placed a groping but apparently deliberate boot on top of his nervous hand. He bit his lip to stifle the instinctive shriek of pain and, looking up in silent protest, he caught a look of contempt in the other's face.

The thin man's companions were professional criminals, successful perhaps, yet basically common thieves. Yet *they* seemed to despise *him* because he was not one of them. It hurt. It was his knowledge, his information that had made it all so simple for them in the past. Any petty crook, any illiterate youth, even a trained chimpanzee, could break into a library or an antiquarian bookshop, where security precautions were invariably something of a joke. The true skill lay in knowing what was worth taking and where it might be found. His partners would be hard put to distinguish a priceless Gutenberg bible from the commonplace Oxford Dictionary.

The thought made him smile involuntarily and rather to his surprise he found his right foot touching the floor. His pre-occupation with them had obliterated his nervousness and he relaxed slightly, determined to regain some of his lost authority.

He walked purposefully to the locked wooden cabinet at the end of the room, framed beneath an imposing gallery with even more shelves. Thousand upon thousand academic and scholarly books stared down at him complacently, as though they *knew* they were safe, that he and his companions were interested only in the valuable antiquarian volumes locked away, among them four magnificent examples of English

6

incunabula. He signalled with an imperious finger for the thugs to force the doors, quickly losing that composure again as they brushed him aside. Nothing had changed; they still regarded him with irritation. So why on earth had they insisted he accompanied them this time? He would be the first to admit he was out of his depth as a cat-burglar . . . they hadn't needed him before . . . why now?

They opened the doors with a minimum of fuss, using what looked like a cold chisel, and a larger pair of metal cutters to slice through the long chains that secured half dozen huge volumes. Despite his dislike of these men he could not help admire their silent efficiency although when he looked again at the chains he could see how ineffective they really were. They started loading the books into a huge rucksack—quickly but with reasonable care—until one, obviously heavier than expected, slipped from a surprised grasp. The covers opened in the down-draught, but the man caught hold of one end and the hinges strained protestingly.

Involuntarily the thin man snatched it from him, shouting far louder than he intended, "Careful! Do you *want* to destroy it? That's 500 years old! Split the spine and it's worthless . . ." He was conscious of wild exaggeration but guessed they would not question his knowledge.

One of them muttered something rude under his breath, but the thin man barely heard. He was conscious now only of the impressive book, more than twelve inches long, in his arms. The mingled smells, peculiar to truly antiquarian books—the mustiness of very old paper and of polished leather—thrilled him and his heart appeared to swell exultantly. He did not need to look at the small title on the spine; he recognised this book from photographs. He was holding a landmark in literary and English printing history.

7

There were probably only a dozen or so copies in the whole of the world and this one was in remarkably good condition for its age; the green morocco binding rubbed and a little slack but the contents practically complete and the splitting or tears at top and bottom of the spine and at one hinge quite minor. He opened the top cover gingerly and inside read:

The Book of Hawking, Hunting and Heraldry. With pounding heart he found the printer's mark and date: St Albans, 1486 and on other leaves numerous woodcuts, and coats of arms in black, red, yellow and blue—the earliest example of colour printing in England. It was known reverently as *The Book of St Albans* because outside London there were only two centres of printing, St Albans and Oxford, but the thin man knew of its other unique features.

The printer, for example, was the fascinating Wynkyn de Worde, one-time schoolmaster, and editor to William Caxton. The thin man's eyes brimmed with emotion as his fingers traced the scratches on the leather binding, wear and tear representing so many generations of appreciative owners and students. This copy was probably worth about £10,000 but the money meant nothing to him, determined to demand the book for himself. He had never thrown his weight about and from the start never become involved in any financial wrangle. He was essentially a scholar, involved merely to help someone else, unconcerned with material gain. The *Book of St Albans* was something else.

His reverie was interrupted as one of the men snatched the book from him and stuffed it into the rucksack. The thin man looked on, distraught, realising that now was not the time to argue with them. They were, after all, in their element and he recognised their authority here as absolute. He moved towards the ladder and their escape route. They would clear up and follow and he didn't want them breathing impatiently down his neck again. It would be bad enough negotiating the roof and the fire escape but the rope ladder looked uninvitingly and extremely precarious. He looked at his watch and was surprised to see that less than ten minutes had elapsed since they had entered the library. He was ready to go but with one hand on the ladder glanced back and was disconcerted to see them adding to their haul with books from an adjoining shelf. Even more upsetting was the way they were so roughly stuffing them on top of the fragile incunabula.

"We don't need those," he instructed. "They're a waste of time."

"Mind your own business," one of them grunted, not bothering to look up.

The festering knot of irritation in his stomach exploded sharply at the contempt in that voice. Both of them—he did not know their names, nor could he tell them apart—behaved as though he was not even there. There were limits to his self-control. "You forget who I am," he warned. "Those books are only excess baggage!"

But they continued filling the rucksack until one of them with an effort lifted it just a few inches off the ground. The thin man could see they were indifferent to his threats and he was wary about antagonising them too much; they looked a violent pair and he had little doubt they were when occasion demanded it. He contented himself with a petulant shrug and a parting thrust; "Very well, if *you* want to lug that ton weight over the roof, that's your funeral!" He turned to go but was arrested by a quick retort from the leader.

"No . . . its your's . . ."

He turned his head and saw them smiling maliciously. Ignore them. He concentrated on the ladder, placing his right foot on the second rung, and started the almost vertical ascent. He had taken only one step when a powerful hand grabbed the seat of his pants and

9

hauled him back. His feet could only have been eighteen inches off the ground but the shock and violence of the attack played havoc with his balance and he sprawled in a heap. The impact jarred his ankles and he caught his right knee a stinging blow on the protruding carved pattern of the nearest bookcase. But the pain was instantly forgotten as he looked up at his attackers, surprised and suddenly terrified. The dislike was mutual but they had been working towards the same end and they had friends in common. What was going on? With parched throat, he mouthed his thoughts: "What's going on? Was that supposed to be a joke?"

The smile left the face of the leader. "No joke, Professor. We're just parting company." The derisory use of the title 'professor', to which he was not entitled, heightened the menace in the voice.

"What . . . what have I done?" he appealed.

They failed to answer. As though by telepathic co-ordination they grabbed him under each arm and lifted him sharply to his feet. Then, with an effort, one of them hauled up the rucksack and together they managed to manhandle it on to his back. The thin man buckled under the weight and he clutched desperately at the ladder for support. It swayed away and lifted him on to his toes but when it returned the men steadied it and he remained upright.

The straps cut sharply into his shoulders and the dead weight placed an intolerable burden on the small of his back. He managed to stay on his feet only by hanging on to the ladder, which, mercifully, did not move again. He shook his head at them faintly. "It's impossible . . . at least take *some* of the books out."

"Sorry, Professor," the leader replied cheerily. "Come on now, we don't know *what* we can do until we try. Let's go . . ." He leapt lightly on to the third rung, leaned over to grab his victim by the collar and pulled.

The thin man had to climb or be choked. All the weight seemed to be concentrated on his back and thighs, so that his lower legs were almost numb. His shoes gripped the floor as though they were magnetised but with enormous concentration he lifted his right foot on to the bottom rung. Distantly conscious of a word of encouragement from somewhere and a sharp push from behind from the second thug, he managed to heave himself up one rung.

The effort was enough to exhaust him and he closed his eyes wearily. He doubted his ability to get anywhere near the top and found it difficult to decide whether the tug at his collar was a help or a hindrance. Each rung seemed to take a superhuman effort and he soon lost count of the steps he had taken . . . all he knew was that the open skylight seemed as far away as ever. Despite his preoccupation the old fears returned. He had to concede that the climber above seemed to hold the ladder more still than it had been during his descent (compared to this, what on earth had he had to worry about then?) but he was considerably more handicapped . . . would the sweat turn into a mini-tidal wave that would send his glasses planing off like a surf-board? Would the rope suddenly snap under the tremendous weight he now represented?

At the halfway stage he looked down and saw the second man was no longer following him. He was standing at a distance and looking up, which was a minor relief. But the tug at his collar was still there. He was now so physically and mentally exhausted that he no longer *cared* whether he survived or fell. A fall from this height would merely mean oblivion and that thought was a welcome one. But the rare editions among the heavy volumes on his back—and one in particular would be damaged, even destroyed, by the impact. It was that fear that kept him going, an automaton, eyes closed, face and body soaked in sweat,

11

determined to move upwards until he could mercifully collapse on the roof. He was aware of a draught, which meant the skylight was only a few feet away. Incredibly the grip was removed from his collar and he risked opening his eyes.

His tormentor grinned down at him. "Well done, Professor. Tell you the truth, I never knew you had it in you. In fact, you've overdone it."

The thin man looked at him blankly. There were two rungs to go. What was the illiterate pig talking about? Two more rungs. He reached up with his right hand.

The man above shook his head. "You don't understand, you poor sod. This is as far as you go." He lifted a foot and thrust it against the thin man's chest.

The eyes of the "professor" widened in alarm. He was too exhausted to resist, arms too drained even to retain their grip. Stiff-legged, he overbalanced and fell head-first backwards. He was also too tired to cry out and when he hit the floor the force was so great that he actually bounced and his spine snapped in two pieces. The rucksack burst open and the books scattered over the library floor.

The man who had remained behind moved to check his pulse and then sprang on to the rope ladder with the agility of a monkey. He did not give the "lost" books a second glance.

ONE

I can't believe anyone actually likes getting out of bed in the morning but on that crisp Autumn day I had good reason for staying under the covers. Laura Cottingham was one hundred and twenty pounds of Woman and if that capital letter seems pretentious I make no apology because looking down at her, even partially covered, was a pretty intoxicating experience. Put another way, she was intoxicatingly pretty. In bed she was as comforting as an electric blanket but a hundred times more versatile; rather like taking a "trip"—with the option, depending on your mood, of tranquilisers or pep pills. But before you get the impression that I'm obsessed with bed, let me make it clear that Laura was highly intelligent and had a bubbling personality that could have made her a movie star overnight, had she been interested.

The sun was streaming through the huge picture window and if I bothered to lift myself into a sitting position, I could enjoy through it the sweeping panorama of green Dorset hills. The house, a rambling six-bedroom Queen Anne structure dating from 1703, faced the village High Street—the front rooms on the ground floor converted into a shop. Very sensibly, it had been built on the brow of a hill, so that the unrestricted view from the back on a clear day commanded more than sixty miles of coastline.

The undulating landscape reminded me of my companion and I stirred restlessly. I couldn't lie in bed all day. For a start I had promised to drive over to the vicarage before opening the shop, to pick up a collection of 17th century theological works the vicar was selling.

Laura was a bad influence. When she came for the weekend I missed my early morning run and barely found even the eleven minutes needed for the Canadian air force exercises I should have done instead.

My restlessness disturbed Laura who looked at her watch and groaned. "It's only . . . God! You're not getting up? It's the middle of the night . . ."

"By London standards, perhaps," I said reasonably. "But when did *you* last see sunshine in the middle of the night? In the country we're very precise about these things . . ."

She groaned again. "God! How bloody boring." She put her head under the covers.

"Anyway, it's all that wine you consumed last night, not lack of sleep," I pointed out, nobly adding, "Stay in bed. Give me half an hour and I'll even bring you up breakfast." The moan from beneath the sheets was undecipherable and I finally made the effort, throwing back the covers on my side of the bed.

But just at that point the phone rang unexpectedly, making us both jump. "God!" she exclaimed, wide-awake.

Since I'm amused at things like people slipping on banana skins I laughed and told her that as a copywriter she ought to extend her vocabulary, suggesting that she might try reading. I thought that was quite witty but had to be quick to avoid the punch she threw in my direction.

"I never want to read another book for the rest of my life. I'm up to there with books," she complained, raising a hand to her chin.

I turned my head to admire her upturned breasts. "Up to where . . ?"

She dived under the covers again. "For heaven's sake, stop that racket."

I picked up the phone and heard Laura sigh with relief. Fully expecting at this unearthly hour on a

Monday morning an apologetic "wrong number", I grunted incoherently into the mouthpiece.

"Matthew Coll?" the caller's voice was unfamiliar but it was obviously no wrong number. "I apologise for ringing so early . . . hope I didn't get you out of bed," he began with just the right blend of sincerity and authority, indicating that he probably wasn't too bothered. "I'd like to drive down from London to see you, so I thought I'd ask if that was convenient before you made any plans for the day."

"I'll be here most of the time. Who is that?"

"My name is Frensham. Wilfred Frensham . . . you may have heard of me?"

I had. Although a newcomer to the antiquarian book business—after little more than six months I was still finding my feet and more preoccupied with basics than trying to infiltrate the Establishment—I could not help but recognise him as the doyen of the trade. Frensham was chairman of an old established antiquarian bookseller's in Grosvenor Square, a firm which frequently made the headlines on the arts pages of the national press for the frequency with which they topped the bids at international auctions. Frensham's, a family business, not only bought the rarest books and manuscripts for themselves and special clients but represented leading literary institutions and libraries in the United Kingdom and the United States. It was no secret that they were backed by a European banking consortium but it was the firm's knowledge and authority that commanded the respect and jealousy of their rivals. As an individual Wilfred Frensham stood head and shoulders above his contemporaries. A former President of the Antiquarian Booksellers Association, he still remained the grey eminence behind their more important committees.

What on earth did he want with me? I could not offer, either from stock or even purchases for immediate resale, the sort of books in which Frenshams dealt. My shop housed a few thousand of what is considered in the trade "good secondhand stock", with a smattering of unspectacular antiquarian material, sufficient to attract the educated browser or a fellow dealer—but never justifying a special 100 miles journey from someone of the stature of Wilfred Frensham. Perhaps he wanted to buy the shop as it stood? While the stock was ordinary by his standards, the house and its setting were unquestionably beautiful. It was, after all, this combination that had proved irresistible to me. But why Wilfred Frensham? If he was by some chance on the verge of retiring he could afford to take a 50-room mansion nearer London, giving him the best of both worlds. One of the attractions to me had been the price and that was because the shop was off the beaten track. But this was all foolish speculation, so I simply asked why he wanted to see me.

He didn't give me that satisfaction. "I'm a little pushed for time now, Mr Coll, but naturally I'll explain when we meet. Could we make it about three?"

When I put the phone down I told Laura the gist of the brief conversation and the reasons for my curiosity. Laura was a brainy girl whose heart only occasionally ruled her head. I was aware that she had entered our more than casual relationship on her terms—which suited me. In fact she came and went as it suited both of us; currently a couple of long weekends a month. She told me to come back to bed. I declined in favour of a shower although I was uneasily aware that at 32 my youth was disappearing at an ever-increasing velocity and that probably I had my priorities wrong.

I should make it clear that I was determined to make a success of the shop. Bookselling fascinated me. I'd had my fill of the London rat race and, having reconciled myself to never being a truly rich man, I was anxious to make a decent living at least and to get some aesthetic

16

satisfaction from the work.

Laura joined me in the shower, claiming that she was demonstrating the fact that she didn't really enjoy lazing in bed. "I can see what draws you," she said mockingly, soaping herself vigorously. "It's the *pace*. All go . . . hot-line from London before breakfast, queues jostling outside before opening time. I just looked out of the window and you'd think it was London sale-time—just *fighting* to get at your . . . er, Trollopes."

"Same to you," I said, prising myself from her soapy grasp and stepping on to the bath mat. "If you really did look out of the window like that we'll have the village bobby paying us a visit."

"What—is he sexually deprived too? Like the rest of you yokels with straw in your hair?"

"You can mock, my love, but there's more to running a country bookshop than opening the doors at ten o'clock. It's relatively easy to *sell* books—the problem is getting them to sell. That's why I have to nip out in half an hour. If I'm not back in time, perhaps you can open up?"

"That's why you asked me down. You're too mean to pay a proper assistant."

"You should be flattered. Pretty girls are a dime a dozen—not girls I'd leave in charge of the shop."

She fluttered her eyelashes with mock modesty. She had dried herself and started to get dressed so I shaved. "Why don't you let me take you away from all this?" she called. It was framed as a joke but she possibly meant it.

Laura earned enough to keep both of us until I could find another job but nothing was going to prise me away from Dorset, at least not until I had made a proper attempt at making a success of the shop. I kept the banter light-hearted. "I've only been here six months; ask me again in another six months."

She put her freshly made-up face round the bathroom door. "If your shaving speed is anything to go by it'd better be six years."

I finished and grabbed a sports shirt—no more morning hassles over formal collar and ties—and led the way downstairs to the kitchen. We worked instinctively as a team preparing the breakfast. "The most common question I'm asked is 'Have you read all those books?'" I told her as we began to eat. "The answer is 'no' but perhaps that's the sort of target I should set myself before thinking of chucking it in?"

Laura laughed. "I really admire your initiative but let's face it, you have the opportunity to do as you like, you've got no ties and responsibilities—not even me. I'm too independent."

It was the first time she had been as frank. I nodded in a matter-of-fact way but said nothing. The arrangement suited me perfectly. Laura was my favourite but not the only occasional boarder.

The shop has enormous charm and character. I can make that claim with all humility because it all happened before I arrived on the scene, in fact, one of my reasons for buying it. The previous owner, one of the grand old men of bookselling—without being in the slightest unkind one could say he was almost a caricature from Dickens—had been here nearly 40 years, including ten of his "retirement". He obviously matched the setting far better than me although in another thirty years perhaps . . ? Desmond Taylor had infused the shop with his own personality but the biggest single contribution had been his discovery of an original open beamed fireplace behind the modern one. The restored fireplace had added an extra dimension and a focus of attention; around it he had placed some book-shelves and above hung a couple of long copper bed-warmers.

There used to be books everywhere but I'd tidied the

18

place up a little although I was fully aware that confusion and unexpected finds are part of the attraction to the bibliophile on virgin territory. I'd added a few old guns to the antique weaponry and hunting horns old Taylor had installed—and the mixture finally looked like a cross between the film set of a Scottish castle and an old coaching inn. The incongruity didn't worry me since many of my customers were overseas tourists who screamed with delight at what they "recognised" as a lost part of olde England. At least the *women* screamed; the men registered their approval with furrowed brows and approving nods.

If I say so myself it's a delightful place, and I never tire of the familiar clichés of congratulation. Even Wilfred Frensham was impressed. He didn't need to introduce himself. Even at first glance this tall and distinguished man could have come only from London—and the West End at that. One's immediate impression was one of elegance. Immaculately dressed and with long silver hair and matching pencil-thin moustache, he was as tall as me, fractionally under six feet, slimly built and handsome in an aesthetic way. I had imagined him to be about sixty and if so he was remarkably well-preserved. His voice was deep and well-modulated.

"Charming place you have here," he said as we shook hands.

"Did you have a pleasant drive?" I asked rather formally, conscious of mouthing platitudes.

"Came on the motorway to save time. Fast but *not* very pleasant. I expect you know a better route."

I offered to provide him with a couple of more interesting alternatives before he left and led the way to my sitting-room at the back. Laura had provided coffee on cue and I introduced them. She was dressed in her 'weekend' clothes, a pair of faded jeans and polo-neck sweater, but she had a flair for making the ordinary look

19

fashionable. Her colouring, particularly the green eyes and chestnut hair, was normally striking but when she smiled the face sparkled and I felt momentarily possessive. Indeed the earlier mood of complacency was disturbed by Frensham's appreciative look and the way she responded to his sophistication. I suddenly realised he was probably not as old as I had assumed. "You bloody smooth bastard," I thought unreasonably and was greatly relieved when she volunteered to keep an eye on the shop.

"You're alone then, most of the time?"

I wasn't sure whether he was referring to the business or my private life. Did I detect a note of condescension? I was beginning to find his composure mildly disconcerting and decided to dispense with the social niceties. "Mr Frensham, hadn't you better tell me why you're here? I'm at loss to understand what it is you want from me or my business."

He sensed the note of antagonism and smiled apologetically. "I'm sorry, Mr Coll. It's not your stock, as you've assumed—although I'm sure you underrate it. It's you, as a person."

His seriousness reassured me. "Nothing we could have discussed on the phone?"

He shook his head. "A matter of extreme confidentiality and rather complicated too. I'm here wearing my Antiquarian Booksellers Association hat. We want to ask you to do something for us. Your initial reaction may be to decline so I wanted to be on hand to present our case."

I was even more bewildered and it must have shown in my expression. A note of embarrassment crept into his voice. "I'm being very obscure, Mr Coll, but please bear with me for a few moments longer. Our interest is not so much to do with your new business—although naturally we hope you'll do well and sooner or later apply for membership of the ABA. It's in your background . . . military intelligence. It was drawn to our attention by a committee member I believe you know—Philip Henrie?" I nodded cautiously and he continued, "Philip volunteered your name at an emergency meeting two days ago. As you can imagine, an emergency meeting is only convened to deal with a very special crisis and decisions reached have little relation to the normal business meetings. Anyway Philip said you were the man we need. Admittedly, he qualified his submission with a proviso that you preferred to forget the past and that we would probably be wasting our time . . ."

"He's probably right," I interrupted, "even though I still don't know what it is you're driving at."

"No doubt you've read in the newspapers and heard on the grapevine about a number of thefts of valuable antiquarian works from special libraries and certain better-known shops?"

I nodded.

"Whatever you know is depressing enough but the fact of the matter is that the robberies have been on a much larger scale than anyone could imagine. We all know that men have been stealing books for almost as long as others have been selling them but this is the first time we have been able to recognise some sort of organised pattern. Over the years we and the Libraries Association have done our best to deter the crooks but we've always been at a tremendous disadvantage."

I raised my eyebrows, merely to encourage him to proceed, but surprisingly he misinterpreted the gesture as one of disagreement and he flushed. Although the inference was unintentional, I was childishly pleased to have punctured his composure. Obviously Frensham was sensitive to implied criticism of the trade establishment and therefore himself.

"That wasn't just sour grapes," he explained hurriedly. "We're in an impossible position because the

21

only practical way to protect valuables is to lock them away. You can do that with jewellery but by the very nature of our vocation *we* can't. Obviously at more affluent or older established firms like my own there is a decent safe, which provides something of a deterrent. Material from our safe is only displayed in the presence of one of my staff. But it is not practical for a library to keep watch on all its researchers and at most universities that includes distinguished academics engaged in original research and making use of rarely consulted source material."

"It *is* a problem," I agreed.

"In the 'good' old days we had to contend with the ingenious amateur who managed to pull something off from time to time but in recent years the professional hoodlums have added a new dimension to the problem. These gangs—attracted by the big money at hand for readily saleable items, such as antiquarian maps—have been into a few of the more exclusive firms and literally cleaned them out. I don't suppose even our safe is much of an obstacle to the really determined professional after a specific item."

"Surely the very valuable material is almost impossible to dispose of? Even a very high class establishment like yours would be somewhat suspicious of someone who walked in with a Gutenberg Bible—no matter how plausible he seemed? You would hardly write out a cheque on the spot . . ."

"Of course we're cautious. Especially so, as we are the ones who usually suffer in the end. If we sell something that turns out to be stolen we have to refund that money and our only recourse is to sue the thief, if he's convicted, in a civil court—when he comes out of prison. You can imgaine what our chances are . . ?"

"You're presumably not covered by insurance?" I enquired.

He laughed humourlessly. "I advise you to look

22

pretty closely at the small print of your own policy, Mr Coll. For the sort of book we're talking about they condescend to cover us if it spends 24 hours of the day in a safe."

"I hadn't realised you were quite so vulnerable."

He nodded. "One has to remember that we are seldom dealing with any one object as exclusive as a painting—at least, not with the printed book. If there are one, two or even half a dozen copies in existence there are records—we usually know who the owners are. But one of twenty or thirty copies surviving from the 15th century can still be exceptionally rare, yet you might have no way of knowing where they all were. If someone turns up with a plausible story, who can be sure whether or not he is respectable? It probably *is* perfectly genuine."

"I don't quite see where I fit in. My military intelligence background is quite unrelated to this sort of thing."

"It's not your experience so much as your aptitude that Philip was talking about," he continued. "Philip said, in the nicest possible way, that you reminded him of a bloodhound and that he wouldn't like to have you on his back."

It was my turn to flush. I didn't like to be reminded of those days and the things I had sometimes had to do in the name of patriotism or sometimes, without loss of conscience, to save my neck. "As Philip anticipated—that's all in the past. I'm a bookseller now and proceeding with caution at that."

"Point taken, Mr Coll. He didn't say what the work was but I'd hazard a guess it was something political. That can be a nasty business, doubly so to a man of integrity and undoubted sensitivity—as any bookseller must be . . ." He broke off and grinned at the obvious flattery. "But when you left the army I understand you worked for the Chronicle group in some special capacity

23

and cleared up a murder case that had the police baffled."

It was hard to resist a smile at the way facts become distorted at third and fourth hand. The "special" assignment had been merely part of my job as personal assistant to Sir Stanley Drummond, chairman of the powerful Daily Chronicle media group, but I didn't want to go into that now. "That was a nasty business too," I conceded. "That's one of the reasons I chucked the job in and came down here. Booksellers don't usually get mixed up in the dirty side of politics or in murder and I'm not abnormally accident-prone."

"I sympathise and I'm sure you've chosen wisely. But if one decides to settle—make one's bed, so to speak— within a certain community, a trade or profession, one expects to take on an obligation to that community—to make a contribution to its well-being; not merely take out whatever you can. Book-stealing is a cancer that affects us all. You may feel somewhat isolated at the moment but sooner or later the ripples will spread out and reach you . . ."

I tried to keep a straight face. "That makes sense. But just what sort of contribution do you expect of me? To imitate Sherlock Holmes?"

"Something like that." He smiled but he wasn't joking.

I returned his smile. "I don't want to be rude, Mr Frensham, but Philip Hendrie has given you a greatly exaggerated impression of my powers of deduction. I'm not a detective *really* . . ."

"That's splitting hairs. The expression Hendrie used was 'man hunter'. We don't need someone to creep around looking at fingerprints through a magnifying glass. The police are perfectly capable so far as routine detection is concerned. Their problem is that thefts have taken place over a wide area, which means that different county forces have been involved—with

24

varying degrees of efficiency and interest. There seems to be no way of *linking* their efforts . . ."

"You want a co-ordinator?"

"The other day I had some young puppy from the Fine Arts Squad in London, young enough to be my grandson, solemnly telling me that there was no chance of finding the stolen books in one particular robbery he was investingating because, as he put it: 'they all end up in the private library of some rich collector who will buy anything stolen if its rare enough . . .' I must confess I told him I'd been in the business since before he was born and I had only met two men from among many thousands of collectors who *might*, just might, fit into that category—and that he'd been reading too much James Bond."

I concurred. "Truth is sometimes stranger than fiction. But it is very unlikely."

"Exactly. What I'm looking for is someone who knows books and more particularly *cares* about them. There *is* a pattern but its only something that one of us would spot."

"Why don't you do the job? You've *forgotten* more about antiquarian books than perhaps I shall ever know . . ."

"I haven't the other skills."

I admitted the proposal was tempting but explained the restrictions of my current business programme and why it was impossible for me to spare the time. It wasn't a question of a fee to cover my time and expenses, so much as one of losing the momentum I had built up.

He had already given the matter some thought. "I wasn't just talking about a contribution from *you*, Mr Coll. We must all make an input in different ways. Some of us lose a lot of money every year by theft and through innocently buying stolen material. I've recommended a levy in terms of stock or money, which would have the effect of keeping you more than fully supplied with the sort of books you need for as long as it takes. That more than takes care of one worry. The other is manpower. We're not, in any case, expecting to uproot you and send you hurtling about the country. There's no reason in fact why you should not be based here and carry on as normally as possible. But for shop hours I can provide a first class assistant at our expense—retired chap who'd grace any bookshop, including my own. Not someone to just sit there and take the money but someone who could help you in every sense of the word—without in any way over-stepping the mark."

"I don't know him?"

"Name is Charlie Appleton. Lives about 30 miles away but during the week we can put him up at that hotel down the road."

"He could stay here—there's a spare room," I volunteered, realising as the words tumbled out that I had inadvertently accepted the assignment.

Frensham smiled. "You won't regret it . . ."

I returned the smile quizzically. "Stop, please, before I'm on my knees thanking you for giving me the opportunity."

"It's we who should thank you for taking what I've said on trust. I'll make it clear now, we're not expecting miracles. If your enquiries lead nowhere I for one will not be terribly surprised. But we've got to do some-thing."

"Fair enough. And I'll accept on condition that I have your word my business will not be allowed to suffer in any way. I won't start until your man Appleton puts in an appearance."

"Excellent. He'll be here tomorrow."

I looked surprised and he laughed apologetically. "I merely asked him to stand by in the hope of your agreement. Does that present any problems?" I shook my head and he continued: "In the interim you can start

26

to familiarize yourself with the facts . . ." He produced a sheaf of papers from a briefcase. "I've also brought some background information on book thefts and what we've done to combat it to date. Among that wodge of papers there's a report of a joint committee set up by ourselves and the Libraries Association."

As he talked I quickly leafed through the reports of the break-ins. In under a month more than a dozen university libraries had been robbed and about half that number of important antiquarian booksellers as well as a couple of private collectors. I was stunned. "I've only heard about three or four at most," I admitted.

"I don't know whether even the police are fully aware of the magnitude of this outbreak . . . there's no formal evidence linking them. But *you* wouldn't have heard because we've managed to keep much of it out of the newspapers."

"What was the point of that?"

"Those who have reason to tighten their security have been fully alerted. A danger of telling all and sundry is that we're drawing attention to our vulnerability. Don't want to tempt fortune any more than we need."

I finished skimming the information he had presented. "I'll study this properly in due course but tell me one thing. Why are you so sure that there's a pattern?"

He stood up. "There had better be! Heaven protect us if we have to contend with a dozen or so professional gangs on the rampage. My theory is based on the timing, or speed of the operation, and the geography. Seems like the work of a small mobile team, directed by someone who knows what to go for . . ."

I stood up and helped him on with the lightweight Italian topcoat—the sort of design I always admire in the shop window but can never afford. "After your comments on my background it would just be my luck if it did turn out to be a politically motivated gang—raising funds by robbing the Establishment," I speculated.

He shrugged. "Can't be ruled out. Although if someone is that dedicated there's more money in robbing banks . . ."

"But more dangerous."

"Don't let's jump to conclusions," we concluded almost in unison, as though we had been thinking on the same lines. But it seemed too serious a matter for either of us to laugh.

We went into the shop where Laura was talking animatedly with a customer, belying her professed lack of interest in books. She completed the sale and extracted a promise from the man to return soon and when he had left I thanked her. She shrugged disparagingly. "It's so easy," she said. "I don't know why you men create all that mystique."

"No mystique," I argued. "It's just that you're such a natural. Wish you'd stay."

She laughed. "Of course . . . for the wages you pay me . . ."

Unaware of Laura's strange sense of humour, Frensham intervened. "I didn't realise you worked for Matthew Coll?"

She played up to him. "Worked? *Exploited* is a more accurate term. Don't let that wide-eyed innocence fool you . . ."

He looked at me and then back to her. "It *doesn't*, Miss Cottingham. I'm entirely on your side."

I raised an eyebrow. "That's a fine start to our association."

At the word 'association' Laura forgot her game. Her face lit up. "So there *was* a business proposition?" Unfortunately when I shook my head she probably didn't believe me; at least she shrugged her shoulders. "I'm only the hired hand . . !"

I promised to tell her later but this time I had put my foot in it because she had jumped to the conclusion that I could not take her into my confidence. With a show of indifference she said it would have to wait because she was in a hurry to get back to town now.

Frensham presented his colours like a knight seeking favours at the joust. "Can I give you a lift back?"

Laura thanked him but said that her own car was parked at the back.

"Then perhaps you can lead the way?" he suggested. "I'm bound to get lost."

I thought that was a bit much. "On the motorway?"

Laura's smile was mocking. "*I* wasn't going to use the motorway going back. I'll want to stop somewhere for a meal; I'm starving. After all, we didn't get much at that workhouse or tramp's rest you took me to at lunchtime."

I groaned inwardly. The publican next door had had a succession of catastrophes over the weekend, including a fault on his gas cooker, which meant he'd been unable to prepare hot food. Laura had been sympathetic at the time but now she was annoyed with me so there was little point in arguing.

Frensham however grabbed at the cue. "Excellent idea. I'm hungry too and we really ought to have the opportunity to talk—we do have quite a lot in common."

"How is that?" I enquired.

He shrugged. "A few moments ago I promised to take an interest in your business and that presumably includes staff relations?" He smiled disarmingly and I could say nothing without appearing to be irrational in my jealousy. I *wasn't* jealous, after all . . . just a little hurt, perhaps?

He shook hands with me and stopped at the door. "Thanks again, Matthew . . . for everything."

Laura put matters in perspective by the way she came

29

over and kissed me but fortunately for my peace of mind my thoughts were already leaping ahead to the investigation with which I'd been entrusted. I could feel the adrenalin beginning to surge through my arteries. I don't know why but the exciting yet reassuring sensation reminded me curiously of an alcoholic taking his first drink after months on the waggon . . .

TWO

Ask the average person what he understands by 'book-stealing' and he will instinctively think of shop-lifting. Before the spate of major losses with which I was concerned he might have been justified. Thousands of books, old and new, are stolen every year, a large proportion probably on sudden impulse. Fascinating how ostensibly honest men and women, law-abiding citizens who would never dream of taking a diamond ring or even a loaf of bread, can be tempted and actually seduced by a book. Bet your life the Freudians would find some sexual connotation although that's neither here nor there.

The trade suffers more than anyone could imagine, and not just financially, because ultimately it rubs off on the attitude of booksellers to quite innocent browsers. I suppose when it happens to me I shall be annoyed but take some consolation (if the loss is not too great!) of knowing that my book or books had found an appreciative home. But we were dealing now with the cold-blooded professional thief, interested only in financial gain. It was highly unlikely that amateurs working for an avaricious collector would be so systematic and certain that they would not be as efficient.

The missing books seemed to have been cunningly selected. For example, they had taken nothing *really* spectacular, the national treasure to be ransomed or sold for a fortune—but which would cause a nationwide hue and cry. Most of them were in the £500 to £5000 category although there were also a few relatively worthless copies, presumably taken in error. But with as many as half a dozen volumes taken from each

31

collection the total cost was now approaching £150,000. The loss might have been even larger because in a couple of cases, both important libraries, records had also disappeared, leaving no evidence that books, possibly stolen, had ever been in their possession. One must remember that in a collection of, say, 200,000 old and very old volumes no librarian can keep tabs on individual titles for which there has been no recent demand. In such circumstances a valuable book can lie gathering dust for years; the only evidence of its existence in that library is the record file index, and if that disappears . . .

The robberies seem to have begun at a college library at Radford; the second came nine days later at Liverpool and the third, the historic Abbey library at Westminster—and this, because of the location, the first to get the attention of the media. From them on, apart from a series of break-ins at leading London booksellers, the attack had been concentrated on libraries and collectors in the south-west.

I had detailed accounts of what had been taken at each site, including information on the books and the way in which they may have been marked or stamped for identification—of value more to their recovery than in trapping the thieves, uless they suddenly got careless, which seemed unlikely and certainly out of character. Frensham had also, very thoroughly, included a considerable amount of information on the patterns of behaviour and characteristics of many booksellers—offbeat ways of identifying stolen property, e.g. prints and maps wrapped in polythene shirt bags could only be the property of dealer X. There were many other "secret" price-marks, some almost as individual as fingerprints!

Thinking of Frensham's thoroughness reminded me that his shop was one of only two which had reported break-ins but had nothing stolen. The thought

32

intrigued. I even wondered for a moment whether *he* might have been behind the robberies and faked evidence of his own "lucky escape" merely to put the police off the scent, but although I had no illusions about anyone's reputation and apparent integrity it simply didn't ring true. Then I remembered the missing library records and had a brain-wave. We had both assumed that the thieves had been foiled by his large safe although they might return later better prepared. But I wondered whether the firm's record books had been locked away and, if not, whether he or his staff had checked them. I rang him at home late that evening, having given him ample time to get back after dining with Laura, and he promised to check first thing in the morning. He admitted they had not considered the possibility at the time; records in ledger form existed since the firm had been founded by his great grandfather in 1831 and would therefore present a formidable task. However he agreed that the information could be imortant and promised that the ledgers would be divided among the senior staff and checked through systematically.

He rang back next day, impressed at my perspicacity. In two ledgers single pages had been carefully torn out, leaving a blank in their sales records for, in one case, four days of November 1904 and in the other, a fortnight in June 1923. The implication was that if Frensham's had sold a particularly valuable book to a college library in those periods there was no longer any evidence to that effect. An unscrupulous dealer could now claim that a disputed book in his possession had an entirely different history or source—known in the trade as the 'provenance'.

Charlie Appleton turned up on time—a big, bluff man of few words—and I liked him instinctively, so that when he had glanced over my stock and muttered his approval I felt childishly pleased. As Frensham had

33

promised, he had a deep appreciation of antiquarian and secondhand books and was more knowledgeable than me so I was able to relax, knowing the shop was in safe hands. I left Charlie getting to know the stock while I returned to the study of the documents Frensham had provided.

It was immediately apparent that visiting the locations of every robbery would be an exhausting business and, if Frensham was correct, I would be lucky to learn anything more than the information we already possessed. Obviously a few visits would be necessary, to see for myself the degree of expertise employed by the thieves in gaining access. Meanwhile I needed to cut through to the heart of the matter by trying to find a link. It was all very well for us to assume that there was a pattern—and I happened to share Frensham's conviction that this was the work of one gang—but it would remain only a theory until we had found the common denominator. An obvious connection were the valuable books to be found at each location. But why *those* unfortunate collections when there were hundreds from which to choose?

The smart London bookshops need not fit into the pattern since anyone who knew anything about antiquarian books and manuscipts could take it for granted that a fair proportion of the stock was always worth taking. Two of them had been leading specialists in antiquarian maps and old prints so it would not have been necessary to have a prior knowledge of what was actually in stock. But most of the victims were university or institutional libraries and it was almost impossible for one person to know what minor treasures each establishment housed. The thought nagged at me. Was there perhaps a reference book? I doubted it but made a note to check. I knew that the weekly and monthly book trade journals did not provide that sort of information and wondered about the libraries . . .

I rang Frensham again. He was out but his nephew Jonathan, the managing director, said that the Libraries Association had a monthly Rare Books Newsletter, which occasionally carried short features on individual member libraries and their more unusual books. He gave me the name of the part-time editor, a librarian with one of the Oxford colleges. Conscious though I was of the need to keep the idea to myself for as long as possible, somewhere along the line I had to trust someone and it seemed too much of a coincidence for the very first person to be approached to be the criminal mastermind we were seeking. I telephoned.

The editor, Harry Worthington, had been doing the job only for the past eleven months but suspected my hunch could be valid. Although he was in the final stages of putting the next issue to press he put the deadline on one side to help me in what he considered to be ultimately in the greater interest of his readers. When I repeated the names of the now depleted libraries he recalled write-ups on a few during his term of office and while we talked he checked his back issues file and located several others. "So far as I can see," he concluded, "that probably leaves only two—Westminster Abbey, and the Radford College library in your neck of the woods."

Radford was a teacher training establishment, housed in what had once been a small monastery. Although it was about 40 miles from my shop I was aware of it as a potential customer and had for some time intended to make myself known. Mentioning my personal interest, I expressed some surprise that the college had anything truly valuable, as opposed to academic material.

"They had a rich benefactor in the 1900s," he explained. "A carpet manufacturer from Devon called Wilfred Potterton, who wanted to leave a lasting memorial to his name. Give the old boy his due, he

35

could have erected a statue in his home town or had a hospital named after him but apart from substantial family bequests he spent the rest on a marvellous collection of incunabula and early illustrated books. Got old man Quaritch to represent him at a couple of the big sales. Cost him about £10,000, which was a lot of money in those days."

"But that rather defeats my theory," I protested. "If all the others had been mentioned in your newsletter they could have been seen by the person who may have organised the robberies—but what about these two?"

He demurred. "Most of us know about the Potterton legacy and similarly the history of the Abbey library. That's obviously better-known; it's even been recorded in booklet form."

"So we would be looking for someone who has access to that sort of information . . . a librarian perhaps?"

There was a momentary silence before he answered, "Much as it pains me to admit it, you're possibly on the right track. You know as well as I do that many collectors are as knowledgeable as the professionals but they are usually specialists. It would take a librarian, even more than a bookseller, to have this breadth of knowledge. Mind you, that still leaves you looking for a needle in a giant haystack."

"What we need is bait," I said, thinking aloud. "Some really choice titbit, completely unguarded, just waiting to be pounced on. Then we spring the trap."

"That's easier said than done. Who, for a start, is going to volunteer to put one of their treasures at risk? Then, how are you going to let our villain know about the bait?"

"That's where you come in," I announced. "When does the next issue appear?"

"Should have been out this week. I'm delaying publication even now by just talking to you."

"I'm sorry but that makes it perfect. We're still in

36

time to announce something in this very issue . . ."

He laughed. "I'd like to help but there are limits. It's bulging at the seams now."

I asked him to take something out to make room for the announcement, that the alternative was to wait a month—which would have the effect of immobilising me. Reluctantly he agreed but pointed out we would still have to seek the co-operation of one of the Association members.

That would have to be left to him, I explained, but suggested that we would be minimising the risk by inventing a collection that did not exist or referring to little-known but genuine items from other collections. "That way the library—and you must have one or two special friends you can trust and who would co-operate—could lock their own stuff away for the duration," I urged.

Worthington was apparently shocked into silence and I wondered whether I had overstepped the mark when rather severely he pointed out that I was asking him to misinform his entire readership on the off-chance of baiting a trap for one person—who might not even read that issue. I argued that the end justified the means and that he could issue a truthful explanation as soon as we felt we were on safe ground. If the experiment failed we would have nothing to hide and he would be at liberty to share with his readers our well-intentioned but ill-fated plot. He refused.

I reminded him that we were arguing about an ethical issue, not an editorial one, and he compromised by promising to consult someone on the Association committee. I asked for a name, telling him I would get Frensham or the President of the ABA to make representations to that person. He was impressed and conceded I might well get my way. To save time I suggested we might proceed on that assumption and he agreed to work on two or three attractive-sounding

37

fabricated titles and to devise a short announcement that the books had been bequeathed to whichever insitutional or college library he could persuade to co-operate. We hoped that this lure provided our thieves with their next port of call.

"I'll be ready," he promised, "but don't take it for granted we'll get authorisation from my committee. You're asking a lot."

I hastened to assure him I was most grateful for his understanding and considerable assistance and would abide by any decision, however unpalatable. But in fact I was smugly confident. He didn't know Frensham's reputation and powers of persuasion.

I put the phone down, greatly pleased with my progress. As several days would elapse before there could be any reaction I thought I might relax and get back to my own business. But the sight of Charlie Appleton dealing with cusomers as though he had been there all his working life reminded me that my presence wasn't particularly necessary. Besides I had the bit between my teeth and was feeling restless. I decided to try another tack. The robberies which fell outside the pattern were from private collections—the first at the home of a Major Harry Edwards, at Dorchester, and the other at Oldham Park, the stately home of Lord Berridge, only a few miles on the other side of Lyme Regis. By country standards we were practically neighbours. A secretary at Oldham Park arranged for me to call next day but Major Edwards would not even see me.

Grudgingly he came to the phone but despite my "credentials" he refused to talk about his loss. His testiness conjured up images of the fanatical collectors with which Frensham's young detective had been obsessed but I had no authority to make him talk. If necessary I could go back and see him later but meanwhile the irritability might have been due to his

38

wariness of the world in general, following the loss of some of his prized possessions. There had been no evidence of forced entry and since the loss had not been detected immediately suspicion might have fallen on dozens of people with access to the house over a two-three month period—members of his own family, servants or even business acquaintances. He told me he was making certain enquiries of his own and prom-ised—a major concession, from his tone—to keep me informed of significant developments. My euphoria after speaking to Worthington had evaporated by the time the Major had finished complaining and I wondered whether to turn Frensham on him. There didn't seem much point. I would get to Edwards later if need be.

Oldham Park had been built five miles from Lyme Regis in 1770 by Robert Adam (or, more likely, one of his pupils) for Henry Berridge, the fourth baronet, one of the most powerful men in the West Country of that period. Ironically, the decline in the Berridge family fortunes could be linked to his death thirteen years later. The name of Berridge had originally come to prominence when the first Henry, one of the small group of loyalists who followed the King's son into exile, was rewarded with a knighthood at the Restoration. But it was his son, William, who really put them on the map when he shrugged off parental disapproval and entered commerce, making a fortune in the process. William had very early on recognised the passionate interest of Charles II and his brother James in restoring the former glory of the British navy and secured himself government contracts to supply timber for H.M. ships. Before long he had cornered the market and muscled in on the rope business too. Charles, the next in line, did not inherit his father's flair and enormous energy but was competent enough to keep the business ticking over until his own second son

Henry entered the scene with the force of a typhoon. At the time of his death the family business was so prosperous that his uninspired descendants were able to coast downhill comfortably for 150 years until it was sold for a mere pittance. Death duties had left the present Lord Berridge relatively impoverished and unable to cope with the huge renovating costs of Oldham Park until, copying his aristocratic contemporaries, he opened the house to the public in the mid 1970s. A succession of family scandals among the dissolute Berridges of the late 19th century immediately made it one of the more interesting stately homes.

Before visiting Oldham Park I did my homework, making various enquiries about the present Henry Berridge, but the picture I had formed was still sketchy. He did not seem to *do* anything and despite the widespread promotion of his home managed to keep himself out of the public eye as much as possible. Henry had inherited the title on the premature death of his father, who had broken his neck in a hunting fall. The accident was a double tragedy because it also cut short a promising riding career for the young heir. The shock seemed to destroy his love of horses and although he could still force himself to ride he no longer enjoyed the rapport that had made him an outstanding point-to-point competitor. He had at one time been a candidate for the Olympic pentathlon team but his strength at riding, pistol-shooting and fencing were not always matched by the required prowess at running and swimming and when those riding skills suddenly deteriorated he disappeared from the international scene. Since the death of his father he had concentrated his energies on game-shooting and—when he could find the money—bigger game abroad.

I don't know that I had any preconceived impression of what he would look like. Perhaps, unfairly but in view of his recent ancestry, I had a hazy Bertie Wooster image although as a crack shot he would hardly sport a monocle. In fact I should have realised that the eyes would be his outstanding feature. It sounds something of a cliché to say that they were "piercing" blue but I had the distinct impression he could focus on me and then on a spot 200 yards directly behind with just a minimal adjustment of his vision. Bionic, that was it! They were almost unreal. The rest of him was undistinguished in comparison; his pleasant features sharp but quite even and his short hair blond, giving him a Nordic look although he did not have the athletic frame that we usually associate with it. There was nothing relaxed about him. Indeed he held his slight body stiffly upright and his jaw slightly raised. I thought at first it was because he was an inch or so shorter than me and had to look up but in due course I noticed that it was an idiosyncracy, as though he was looking down his nose at the world.

As it happened my close study was rather wasted because at the outset he made it clear he knew little about his library, other than that it had been started by his great-great-grandfather, who had been something of a scholar. "My father took an interest," he explained. "In fact he had been to a sale at Sotheby's only the day before he was killed. In the circumstances the collection hasn't changed much since that day although my wife does keep an eye on things—that's how we discovered there had been a few stolen . . ."

"Would it be possible for me to talk with her?" I asked.

"Precisely," he replied, looking as though I had said something idiotic. "She was supposed to *be* here. I'm already late for a meeting." He looked at me accusingly, as though he was being detained against his will.

I had no desire to make small talk so I suggested that if *he* had no objection I would amuse myself in the library until his wife appeared. Berridge beamed expansively at me. "Very thoughtful of you, old chap. I don't want to be rude but I know absolutely nothing about the books." Now that he had been let off the hook, he visibly relaxed and came closer. His manner now verged on the friendly. "I didn't realise the Antique Book Society had a branch on our doorstep. Thought it all happened in London . . ." he said.

"It does," I replied, not bothering to correct his stab at the Association's name. "I'm not even a member . . . more what you might call a consultant in this field. Actually I run a bookshop in Ardley, just the other side of Lyme Regis."

The disappointment showed when I mentioned the shop. An official or committee member of an august body such as the ABA was one thing but the proprietor of a small country bookshop was little more than a local trandesman—with whom, it was obvious, he had little in common. He quickly recovered his poise and like a born gentleman endeavoured to maintain the friendly facade by asking if I had any books on guns or hunting. He didn't expect an affirmative and when I said that I had his enthusiasm returned.

"I don't remember the titles," I said, "but I must have half a dozen on shooting. One I recall is Burrard's *The Modern Shotgun*, because it is in three fine volumes . . . but why don't you pop in and see for yourself? There's also a small section on hunting, including a few old prints, so I'm sure you wouldn't be wasting your time."

His face lit up. I could see he wasn't just being polite now. "I'm glad I asked," he conceded. "I often pop into Lyme Regis."

I advised him to ring first and I would try to be at the shop to discuss the books in question although it occurred to me that Charlie Appleton would probably know more about them than I did.

By the time his wife arrived he seemed to have

42

forgotten his pressing appointment but he pulled himself together, introduced us formally and was off. I had prepared myself for the meeting by checking on his background but had not bothered to enquire about Lady Berridge. So I was unprepared for a custodian like her. I quite clearly remember involuntarily whistling through my teeth and when she approached with outstretched hand and our eyes met my heart seemed to skip a beat. Sounds corny but that's exactly what happened. I had never been short of women friends and Laura was an eye-catcher but Caroline Berridge was something different. Since the two are the only comparison I can make, let's say that in art terms she was a beautiful original and Laura the reproduction—which is probably unfair since Laura's intelligence and personality were part of her attraction. Indeed nine men out of ten would have preferred Laura, but despite the popular view that sexual attraction is like chemistry; I defy anyone to quantify it. In these matters logic flies out of the window.

If one attempted to 'type' her one would call Caroline aristocratic. She was dressed simply in a cashmere twin-set and tweed skirt and her only jewellery was a single row of pearls. Her face was thin and oval-shaped, wide forehead tapering to a small chin. Her dark eyes were deep set and highlighted by long, lustrous lashes and a small acquiline nose. The hair was soft and brown and tied in a severe bun at the back. Her lips were thinner than I normally like and, as lipstick was the only cosmetic she appeared to use, her mouth, accentuated by the scarlet splash of colour, seemed over-large framed in such a narrow jawline. But criticism of features in isolation is ridiculous since the sum of the parts, so to speak, was to me perfection.

Her grip was firm and unselfconscious and she was obviously unaware of the effect she had on me. When Lord Berridge had gone she took me into the library and gave me a detailed account of the loss, confirming what I already knew and embroidering areas covered only lightly in Frensham's report. Unlike the thefts from Major Edward's collection, this appeared to have occurred during a break-in two months before. Again the operation had been carried out professionally; nothing, apart from selected books, had been stolen and no damage had been done, apart from a small pane of glass which had been broken to gain entry to the house via the servant's quarters to which the burglar alarm system did not extend.

The rooms in the house were enormous, the inheritance of a past age when the summers might have been idyllic but the winters a nightmare. Even now, with an extensivce central heating system, the temperature was still fractionally low by modern standards of comfort. However when I was shown into the library these mundane thoughts were swept away. Ranged in open oak bookshelves reaching almost to the ceiling—twice the height of the average home—must have been more than 20,000 antiquarian books. I doubted whether there was a single cloth-bound volume, except perhaps for reference purposes. The immediate impression was one of an apparently huge expanse of leather, calf, pigskin, morocco, in one harmonious blend of browns from beige to the warmest chocolate, highlighted by gilt decoration on the spines.

My admiration must have shown because Lady Berridge asked me to take as long as I wanted. But I pulled myself together, saying I would prefer to come back some other time. "As a bookseller I'm absolutely green with envy," I admitted. "Every minute I stand here is like turning the screw . . ."

She laughed. "You're welcome to come back at any time," she added, drawing my attention to a few of her favourites. I was impressed by her knowledge of old books but she brushed my compliments aside with no hint of false modesty, confessing that she had befriended a couple of librarians and tried to pick their brains whenever possible. "I don't think there's anything wrong in that," she said. "Now that we have met I hope you won't be offended if I try to learn from you too . . ?"

She had said nothing to raise my hopes and I would not normally dream of becoming involved with married women, yet my heart leapt at the prospect. It was probably the attraction of the unattainable—the grass always being greener on the other side of the fence. I replied that I would be delighted to offer advice at any time, conscious that for the first time I had not qualified the offer with an admission that I had only been in the business full-time for six months. Embarrassing, even admitting it to myself. I was not normally prone to vanity.

Over coffee in the drawing-room she asked about my investigation and volunteered her own assistance. "It probably sounds presumptuous," she said earnestly, "when you have the resources of the ABA behind you but I do have a wide range of contacts through my work and I would be happy to put them at your disposal . . ."

I admitted I was in the preliminary stages of the enquiry and would be pleased to call on her later should I require help. First, I explained, I was more concerned with establishing the thieves' pattern.

The rapport between us was established by the time we had finished coffee. We began to talk generally and soon about ourselves. Books were of course the catalyst and after I had related my account of disillusionment with Fleet Street and the blind leap into the world of antiquarian books it seemed perfectly natural to ask about her interest in books. I admitted I had checked up on Lord Berridge and stupidly overlooked her and she was amused at my industriousness.

"There's nothing to know. I'm not very interesting—

really only an extension of my husband," she said. "We split the responsibilities of administering Oldham Park. He looks after the small farm we have on the estate and the general finances and I do the things I *like* doing—such as looking after the library and helping to attract visitors to the house."

"That's surely very important and time-consuming," I said.

She shook her head. "We have an estate manager and a full-time secretary—so neither of us is bogged down with detail. I'm more or less an ideas woman. I *supervise* the advertising, for example. We have an agency that does all the creative work and prepares the media schedule. I just say 'Yes, that's nice' or 'Shall we move that comma, perhaps?' . . ."

I suspected she was being modest. Despite the slight case of infatuation I was still capable of assessing her dispassionately. From a thirty minute conversation I would have said that Caroline Berridge was a highly intelligent woman, one who did not merely react to situations. I could sense that she generated activity, controlled situations in the same way (I realised quite contentedly) she had probably controlled our conversation although I could not be sure of that.

As we shook hands before parting she looked at me earnestly. "You have a very reassuring effect on people, Mr Coll," she declared. "I get the feeling the investigation is in good hands and that we're going to be friends. Do please call again—you don't need the enquiry as an excuse."

I promised I would keep in touch and meant it. But as I walked down the drive towards my old Citroen my eyes were drawn to a new left-hand drive Aston Martin. It had not been there when I arrived and since Lord Berridge had gone I presumed it belonged to Caroline. Suddenly I saw things in perspective. We were in different leagues. Only a couple of days before, I had said much the same thing to Laura, admitting that I was not prepared to move out of mine. Nothing had happened or could happen to change that . . .

THREE

I was in a complacent mood next morning, setting off
for Radford, a pleasant drive through country lanes,
and for part of the way, if I wanted to make a slight
detour, alongside the River Ard. Worthington had
telephoned the good news that our fake entry had been
approved and that the issue had already gone to press.
With a small and uncomplicated print run, copies
would be despatched to members within 36 hours. I had
prepared a list of out-of-print books on education and
the history of education to offer the librarian at
Radford, most of which relevant to some aspect of their
courses—so, either way, I was unlikely to be wasting
the journey.

The librarian, Edward Heyman, had sounded
helpful on the phone and had endeared himself to me be
expressing an initial interest in the list I was bringing.
The friendliness was consistent and tea and biscuits
were ready on my arrival. Heyman perused my list
quickly, nodded his head approvingly a couple of times,
and then called an assistant to check it against their
stock records. "That way we can place an order by the
time you leave, Mr Coll," he said. "Your visit is
fortuitous. What a pity it needed the robbery to bring us
together."

His manner was cordial but his voice was flat and
expressionless, devoid of light and shade, like a recorded
message or a railway station announcer, although when
he was enthused he moved his head and body quite
animatedly. Indeed Heyman was a peculiar-looking
man, probably in his early fifties, extremely emaciated,
with a small intelligent face dominated by steel-framed

48

spectacles so large they could have passed for a comedian's props. He was a wiry, restless man, burning up energy as quickly as the cigarettes fast reduced to stubs in his overflowing ash-tray. I had no doubt it had been empty and clean when the library opened for the day yet by mid-morning there must have been fifteen stubs, many only half smoked. As a 'reformed' smoker I found the habit distasteful yet strangely enough not him. Cigarettes seemed to be a part of his personality, as much as his rather nondescript mode of dress, and I was scarcely conscious of the smoke and smell of tobacco.

He fascinated me. Sharp as a ferret but with an air of authority immediately apparent to another bibliophile. Whether he would have had the same effect on an 'outsider' I wouldn't know but to me he was the typical book scholar and as such worthy of respect. I'm biased, admittedly, but I warmed to him and found myself telling him about my recent history and the shop at Ardley. He had known my predecessor and congratulated me on my initiative.

"I would never have the nerve to go into business on my own," he said. "As an academic I know what the books are worth but I have no commercial judgement. I would either lack the guts to fight it out at the auction in case I was spending too much and would be stuck with an overpriced piece of deadwood—or my heart would completely rule my head and I'd buy at *any* price and to hell with the profit or loss . . ."

I laughed sympathetically. "At my level of buying it's seldom that dramatic. I know the sort of books I can sell and the prices I can ask and that dictates the price I pay. They're not usually worth fighting over."

He wagged his finger disapprovingly. "If you'll permit a word of advice from someone who has been around for a long time: the really great booksellers don't limit their horizons. They frequently buy above their

49

means, in the knowledge that by biding their time they will eventually make a handsome profit."

I conceded the point. "I've already been given similar advice. No doubt I'll start to flex my muscles when I begin to feel I know what I'm doing."

"Of course you will!" he announced confidently. "It's easy for me to talk. I have the best of both worlds— all the beautiful books I could want, never having to worry about selling them and equally never having to worry if we want to buy. Within limits the money is usually there."

I told him I had heard about the Potterton legacy. His face glowed and he spent the next ten minutes describing the collection before showing me where they were housed. "It was obviously the incunabula that attracted the thieves," he said as he led me through three shelf-lined rooms into an inner sanctum. "Luckily for us they set off the alarm before they could complete the job and they made off with only three of our prized possessions, when they might have taken all eight. It's a toss-up as to which were the more valuable in the open market but one of those that were taken is my personal favourite, the *Songes and Sonettes* of Henry Howard, a 1559 5th edition of what is probably the first collection of lyric poetry in modern English. Howard, or the *Lord Haward*, as they called him, was no great shakes as a poet but its very unsophistication and what the book represents are what make it so dear to me."

He stopped at a glass-sided cabinet 4ft tall by 6ft long and 3ft wide. It was raised on short legs at the corners about six inches above the carpet. The books were displayed flat, with long descriptions alongside, on the three glass shelves. I slid open one of the two glass panels at the back to get at the books and put my arm through to get a better impression of their accessibility. "Where were the three that were taken?" I asked.

He pointed to the top shelf. "They were obviously

the most conveniently placed. Probably didn't have time to get the others."

There was no sign of the alarm but, running my fingers along the underside of the cabinet, I felt the socket of a button that would be depressed when the door was shut. It was in the 'up' position now and when I closed the sliding door it clicked down again. What puzzled me was, if our theory about a professional gang was correct, why had they not spotted a protruding button? Perhaps I was giving them credit for experience or intuition they did not possess? If crooks had no shortcomings at all they would never be caught.

"Is this the only showcase protected by an alarm bell?" I enquired.

He nodded. "These systems are quite expensive and there's nothing else here that justifies it."

"That's if you're talking about rare books. But the so-called 'ordinary' stuff you've got in your library is not be be sneezed at. If someone turned up with a lorry and cleared the lot they'd have quite a useful haul. It's happened before. I would have thought an alarm at the front entrance would be useful."

He shrugged. "You're right but where does one stop? This is not the Bank of England. Besides, every book out there is marked and identifiable as ours. I remember an incident of a lorry being used but you have to bear in mind that there is usually someone connected with the college wandering about the grounds, even students sneaking in after hours. Thieves breaking in to the library would have to use considerable stealth."

I accepted the point and my thoughts returned to the stolen incunabula. "You said the books out there are all marked. That presumably applies to the books in this cabinet and those that were taken?"

His head almost jerked away from my questioning gaze and he walked over to an ashtray to stub out his half smoked cigarette. His movements were twitchy

51

and he looked up at me blankly for a second before realising what he had done—actually put out a cigarette before lighting another. He took a pack from his jacket pocket and lit a fresh one absent-mindedly, adding the match to the ash tray. Then he smiled apologetically. "You can see I have something on my conscience," he said, starting to move about again agitatedly.

"They *weren't* marked," I answered myself, making a statement rather than a question.

He grimaced sadly. "To me those books are the most beautiful objects on earth. To mark them with indelible inks or even perforations is sacrilege. There's no question they *should* have been marked but I foolishly assumed the cabinet was safe enough."

I felt sorry for him. The damage was done now. I returned my attention to the cabinet. "Does the bell just ring here—or is it linked to the police station?"

"Just here but it's pretty loud. We can hear it quite clearly from the main building."

"You live here all the time?"

"During the week. I have a flat at Lyme Regis where I stay at weekends and during the vacation periods."

"But you were here when it happened . . . in the early hours, I believe?"

"I have a built-in alarm in my head," he replied. "I'm sure I'd wake up even if this alarm failed to function but it did and I must have been out of bed in a flash. I dialled 999, put on my slippers and dressing-gown and ran over here. I was so distraught I didn't even bring my cigarettes." He laughed at his own joke and I smiled understandingly.

"So you were first on the scene . . ?"

"Only by a short head. One of my colleagues was hot on my tail and he's quite a bit younger so we arrived almost together. There was no sign of the intruders but I made straight for the cabinet and found it as it is now, door open and the books on the top gone."

"How did they break in, by the way? And get out? One of these windows?"

"We don't think so. This is the second floor and the windows are overlooked. The police thought it was through the front door . . . probably had a set of skeleton keys."

I studied the cabinet again, searching for inspiration and wishing I had some training in basic detective work. It seemed to return my stare glassily. I got down on my hands and knees and looked underneath at the alarm mechanism. Alongside the button I could see an inset switch turned to the off position. I withdrew my head and looked up at him. "Presumably, someone switches this on at night and off again in the morning?" I enquired.

"The last to leave and the first to arrive."

"Do you remember who switched it on that night?"

He sucked in the tobacco smoke noisily as an expression of his impatience. "Really, Mr Coll. We've been through this once with the police. I don't quite see the point since there's no question the alarm bell *did* go off."

I apologised. "I was really thinking aloud. Trying to establish a picture of the normal routine. It's not important."

He was mollified. "Actually it was me. It usually is. As head of the department there's usually more to keep me burning the midnight oil."

I stood up and counted on my fingers, listing his nightly procedure as I visualised it. "You clear your desk, come in here, make sure the cabinet is shut and put the switch to the on position. Then presumably you turn out the lights in here and then in the other rooms in sequence as you go out . . ?"

He nodded.

"And when you burst in here that night the lights were on or off?"

"The place was in darkness. There are no blinds and even the light of a torch could be seen outside. There was a little light from the moon."

I was still troubled by the intruders' carelessness but I got no help from staring at the cabinet. I was reluctant to leave but Heyman was beginning to look at his watch pointedly and eventually he broke the spell by suggesting we go and see if his assistant had finished with my list of quotes. I was pleased to see that sixteen titles had been ticked off, including several scarce items priced accordingly, so that I would be invoicing them for nearly £100—not a bad morning's business.

We shook hands warmly and I promised to despatch the ordered books by post within a day or two. It was not until I had returned to the car and looked back at the college and the library annexe protruding at right angles from the main building that the nagging worry about the alarm swam to the surface of my subconscious. I had a mental picture of wire cutters slicing through a circuit . . . another of a gloved hand removing a fuse from the junction box, superimposed by the same hand pushing the mains switch to the off position, plunging the building into darkness. The picture rang an alarm bell in my own head although I was unable yet to see any direct connection. But it worried me enough to go back and check. On the way I passed the caretaker's office and, introducing myself, asked where the control box for the main electricity supply to the library was located. He showed me . . . a row of boxes inside a cupboard clearly marked 'Danger: Electricity', just inside the front entrance. It beat me how intruders professional enough to break in quietly and without being seen and certainly aware of the risk of alarms could fail to see the cupboard and automatically switch everything off. The contradiction nagged at me all the way home.

54

Worthington sent me a copy of the newsletter and on page two I read with delight:

"Reading University's collection of English and German incunabula has been doubled by a bequest in the will of the late Arthur Guildham, the pottery manufacturer, which includes his private collection of early illustrated books and a small sum for their upkeep. Highlights from the Guildham collection include:

"Schedel (Hartmann) *Liber Chronicarum*, first edition, folio, Nuremberg, A Koberger 1493. Over 2500 woodcut illustrations in text, some double page by Wohlgemuth and Pleydenwurff. First large initial of text in red, blue and green with ornamental pen work down inner margin.

"Leopold (Duke of Austria) *Compilatio de Astrorum Scientia Decem Continens Tractatus*, first edition, Augsberg, Erhard Ratdolt, 1489. Woodcut astrological diagrams and illustrations including two diagrams in red and black, most woodcut initials and some illustrations partly hand-coloured.

"Lichtenberger (Johann), *Die Weissagunge* . . . *Deudsch* (by Stephan Rodt) . . . *Sampt Einer Nutzlichen Vorrede Und Interricht D Martini Luthers*, Wittemberg, H Lufft, 1527. Luther's interest in this book was because Lichtenberger had foretold the Peasant's War, and that the persecution of the clergy would be followed by a period of calm—which he believed to be dangerous and mistaken."

I rang Worthington to congratulate him on his ingenuity. "Wouldn't mind stealing them myself—if I could be sure they existed," I told him.

He was pleased with himself. "Oh they do, although I'm not quite sure where one could find copies. I thought it was too risky fabricating titles, because we may well be dealing with someone who knows more than us. Anyway I'm friendly with the librarian and he's had a word with the local police, so let's cross our fingers and hope nothing goes wrong."

I said I was tempted to make myself known and go up to Reading but thought it was a bit pointless camping out on the premises on spec for an indefinite period.

Worthington agreed. "Besides, with any luck, we might get a lead first," he pointed out. "Ray Jennings has promised to let me know about every enquiry, no matter how innocent. I told him we want to know even about calls from his pals. Said we couldn't rule out anyone."

I thanked him again and waited impatiently for a reaction. I dared not leave the shop in case Worthington or his friend rang and I found it hard to bury myself in the shop's routine activities. I was conscious of getting under Charlie Appleton's feet so I sent him on a buying mission, utilising some of the funds and goodwill the ABA had promised. On Saturday I had a call from Laura, offering to drive down, but I was feeling restless and put her off.

It was three days—the following Tuesday—before Mr Jennings phoned. He was quite apologetic and doubted whether his news was of any significance but he was reporting as promised. "It's early days. The newsletter was sent printed matter rate, which means that some of the Association members farther afield don't get their copies for a week or so. But I've had two phone calls already. Neither is likely to be of interest to you because they merely rang to congratulate us on our good fortune . . ."

"On the contrary, everything and anything could be of interest."

He hesitated. "I must say I feel a bit of a shit. These men are friends. Even when I tell them the truth later they'll be annoyed that I didn't see fit to take them into my confidence."

I assured him that I had my reasons and that he could claim that he had been acting under instructions from the Association.

He was still unhappy but kept his promise. "The first was Stuart Thornton from St Hugh's, Manchester. He wanted to know how and why we had been singled out. Complained he never gets left a thing. The other was from Eddie Heyman at Radford . . ."

My heart leapt and dipped again. I knew in my heart that it was more than a coincidence yet I did not want to believe Heyman was a crook. I was jumping to conclusions, admittedly, but his call to Reading within possibly minutes of receiving the newsletter had to be significant. I enquired about his reasons.

"He was interested in some of the books," said Jennings. "You may not know but he's a specialist in incunabula and he was interested in the provenance of a couple. Eddie is a mine of information and you don't acquire that sort of reputation without having an insatiable appetite for facts and figures."

Insatiable appetite for the books themselves? I wondered, recalling the uncharacteristic carelessness of the Radford thieves and Heyman's apparent naivety at not marking his most valuable books. But a naive or foolish oversight did not make him a criminal. I was confused.

A strange voice at my ear enquiring if I was still there brought me out of my daydreams. I apologised to Jennings, thanked him for his help and asked to be kept informed of all further calls. But as I replaced the receiver I was preoccupied with Heyman. I dutifully made a note about Thornton's call but I had a feeling that his reaction had genuinely been that of a friend and any further enquiries would lead to a dead end. Heyman was another matter. I had nothing that amounted to evidence by police standards yet I wanted to confront him to see his reaction to the new questions I needed to pose.

I picked up the phone again, dialled the number for

Heyman's direct line and he answered. He was friendly, jumping to the conclusion that I was enquiring about the safe arrival of my books. "The invoice is being processed for payment—so you'll get a cheque within a fortnight or so."

I squirmed at the deception. "Thanks. Actually I wanted to see you again about the robbery . . . just a few points I want to double-check."

There was a momentary silence at the other end. "Fire away then," he said eventually. His voice had a metallic note that sounded cold and unfriendly.

"No. I need to come up there," I explained. "Nothing to worry about. What about tomorrow morning?"

The tone hardened even more. "Forty miles here—and forty miles back again, just to *check* something? Are you being quite open with me, Mr Coll?"

"Look, I have a job to do. I don't like being evasive or keeping you in the dark but please take my word for it, I do need to come up to Radford."

"Very well," he said tersely, "but I'm too busy this week."

I sighed. "Mr Heyman, you've been very courteous to me. I don't want to spoil a pleasant relationship but if necessary I'll approach the College principal."

"And say what?" The voice was defiant.

"That I'm not entirely satisfied with the account I have been given about the robbery."

I could visualise him puffing anxiously at his cigarette, restricted by the phone from pacing about. "You must do as you think fit," he replied eventually.

"Come now," I snapped. "All I'm asking for is half an hour of your time. Is that so much?"

He appeared to reconsider. "I can't see you tomorrow. Perhaps we can make it Thursday morning, although . . ."

I didn't give him a chance to reconsider, telling him

that was fine and putting the phone down.

An advantage of living in the country is that unless you are unfortunate enough to be sited on a major holiday route it presents an opportunity to recapture some of the lost pleasures of driving. Even without motorways the relative absence of traffic means shorter time between distances, without a proportionate increase in the risk factor. Even on a wet blustery day I looked forward to the attractive scenery on route to Radford. Whether it was still the novelty factor or not, I was captivated by the whole of Dorset and South Devon and making a slight detour to take in parts of the lovely Ard valley was more than worth the extra mileage.

After a restless night I had still not resolved my strategy for interrogating Heyman. Even Frensham, on the phone, had agreed it was a predicament. He concurred with my assumption of Heyman's involvement in a conspiracy of some sort but shared my view that openly accusing a highly respected librarian would be irresponsible. How I manoeuvred Heyman into trapping himself he conveniently left to me. I was so engrossed in the problem, rehearsing a number of possible gambits, that the point of taking a more beautiful route was rather lost. In fact I was oblivious to the landscape I admired so much and only came out of my trance as the Citroen skidded very slightly on the wet road surface when apparently I took a bend too fast for this stretch of road. I lifted my foot off the accelerator and determinedly took a greater interest in my surroundings.

In my windscreen mirror I was rather surprised to see a dark blue Jaguar 4.2 saloon about 30 yards behind and gaining imperceptibly now that I had reduced speed. Surprised because I thought I had noticed the same car in Ardley High Street, and then to find it behind me, way off the beaten track, and travelling much faster

59

than is customary in these parts.

I studied the occupants in my mirror; two men, the driver, a scrawny blond-haired youth, probably no more than 19, and his companion older and thickset. I was particularly conscious of the driver because he seemed to be very young to be driving such a powerful car, a saloon at that, and wondered what sort of insurance he carried? I was travelling at 50 m.p.h., fast enough in these country lanes, and as the Jag crept nearer I decided to let him pass. "Mad bastard," I thought, inconsistently since I had been matching that speed only a few moments before.

I had a second surprise in store because the Jag made no effort to pass, remaining about ten yards from my tail. Admittedly, the road was narrow and winding but it was also completely deserted and the youngster behind that steering-wheel didn't seem the over-cautious sort. I looked at them again in my mirror but they continued to look straight ahead so I mentally shrugged and ignored them for a while. About three miles further along the road ran parallel to the river which, following the rain of the past few days, was swollen and looking its best. Along this section it was no more than ten feet across in places, separated from the road by sweeping grass banks another fifteen or so feet wide. A long stretch of trees, some in advanced stages of Dutch elm disease, seemed to form a guard of honour on either side of the river, their gauntness against the black river adding a wintry touch to the setting. In a couple of month's time the road would be icy and motorists would be warned to drive carefully but normally the river was set back far enough not to present a hazard unless one was drunk or driving recklessly.

As the thought flickered across my mind I glanced back at the Jag in time to see the driver look in his own mirror—apparently checking to see there was no-one behind—and then back at me. This time he looked straight at me and simultaneously the Jag started to accelerate. Instinct made me put my right foot down hard. The adrenalin rose in tandem with the speedometer as the Citroen leapt forward and I hoped no other car would suddenly appear ahead to complicate matters. At 70 m.p.h. the Jag was still gaining and gradually pulled out to overtake. All the time I was very conscious of the river and those dangerous trees flashing by on my left and began to wonder if he intended to force me off the road. Desperately I pressed the accelerator to the floor and the Citroen moved ahead again.

This time I took a good look at the number plate. I didn't really know how that was going to benefit me but I was feeling angry enough to report the driver as soon as the river had been left behind and I could safely stop. I concentrated on the white plate and black figures and managed to read W A R, which was easy to remember, and the number 4 4 6 S, before he closed the gap again.

It dawned on me suddenly that I might simply stop and he would go rushing by without a backward glance. Instinctively I eased my foot off the accelerator, gesturing with my right hand for him to pass. But when he did draw alongside the occupants looked in my direction and I realised my original concern had been justified. I slammed on the brakes, praying the wheels would not lock, only a split second before the faster Jag veered to the left to force me off the road. Travelling at that speed and surprised at not making contact, the driver failed to straighten up in time and his own nearside wheels left the road. The difference in the two surfaces, with the soft turf several inches lower than the road, caused him to struggle to control the Jag and he slowed to a halt.

With the bonus of those few seconds I shot past them again but the respite was short-lived. After a hundred yards or so they were on my tail again and gaining. I knew I could not outrun the Jag and thought I might endeavour to outmanoeuvre them by using every inch of the road but the young man was a natural driver. I calculated that if he caught the Citroen off balance and I lost control of the steering the prospects of survival were bleak—on either side of the road. To the right was a high-banked ditch, topped by tree-lined hedges, and to the left the river, separated by the tempting fifteen foot strip of bank. Providing I could avoid the river itself and the trees dotted along the edge, it was the less forbidding prospect.

Even as I made the evaluation the Jag was abreast. To avoid an impact with the heavier car I turned my wheel to the left and hurtled off the road. Of course I should have realised that at that speed a fifteen foot 'safety barrier' was nothing. As the river rushed towards me I panicked momentarily. I applied the brakes in mid-air and the locked wheels skidded off the wet grass, shooting the car towards the water. I remember being hugely relieved that no tree blocked our path because, having left the road at 60 m.p.h. with only the slightest interruption of that momentum, the impact would have been crushing. As it was, the noise of hitting the water was deafening but my seat-belt prevented violent contact with the windscreen.

The car entered the river almost upright but as the nose tilted down we sank very slowly at an angle while the water crept through narrow apertures in the floor and through the doors. I had a horrible suspicion that the water at this point was deeper than the height of the car and that we would soon be completely immersed. But this time I did not lose my head, which was probably something to do with my anger at the occupants of the Jag who had forced me off the road. Presumably it had given them some nefarious thrill; I had heard about that sort of thing being popular in

France in the 1960s. I wound up the windows, waiting anxiously for the added weight of the water creeping in to take the car to the bottom. I knew it would not be possible to open any of the doors until the pressures on either side were the same; in other words, not until the water inside had almost reached the roof.

My stomach churned anxiously as the water rose—it seemed to take an eternity although it was really rushing in—above my waist and it was as much as I could do not to try to force the door prematurely. However I knew there was little point in expending my energies at this stage and contented myself by unfastening the seat-belt and testing the lock on my side to ensure it had not jammed. When the water had reached my neck I decided not to wait any longer and, taking a deep breath, I opened the door. It was like pushing against thick treacle but I was desperate enough to force my way through a brick wall and I soon found enough room to squeeze through. Then I merely had to stretch up, and my head broke the surface. Treading water I took a deep breath and looked around for the Jag or its occupants. I didn't really expect them to be there still but I hoped they would be, feeling indignant enough to take them both on. Honour would not be satisfied until they were in the river too.

Of course there was no sign of them—nor anyone else. I swam to the side, hauled myself out with an effort, and walked to the road. They had chosen their spot well; there were still no cars in sight. On this deserted route I could wait for an hour or more in wet clothes and I was already beginning to shiver, so I cut across the fields to a farmhouse in the distance. I suddenly felt very tired, no doubt something to do with delayed shock, but drew on my reserves of energy to jog in an effort to get warm. I kept my mind on practicalities—the need to ring the police, the A.A., Charlie Appleton . . . Where on earth was I going to find dry

63

clothes? And the car? It could hardly be driven out of the river. What a mess . . . I felt very sorry for myself. Edward Heyman was temporarily forgotten.

FOUR

Normally in the passage of time a nightmarish experience is concertinaed into a split second interlude. The rest of that interminable day, however, will be etched minute by minute in my memory for all time. The ordeal was softened only by the common sense and hospitality of John Dickens, the elderly farmer onto whose land I had stumbled and to whom I will be eternally grateful. The phone calls were made for me as I soaked in a hot bath, drinking a cup of strong tea, and without a moment's hesitation John not only provided fresh clothing of his own but drove me back to Ardley. The local constable had treated my story with some diffidence despite the fact I was able to give him reasonably detailed descriptions and part of the registration number of the other car. It was only several hours later, when they had discovered the Jaguar had been stolen that morning from Bournemouth, that they started to take me seriously.

Later that afternoon I had a visit at the shop from a Detective-Inspector Murdoch, a tall, craggy individual in the shapeless tweed suit with which one usually identifies the plain-clothes country policeman. He had twinkling, shrewd blue eyes beneath shaggy eyebrows and when he smiled the eyes practically disappeared under the heavy blond thatch above. By that time I'd had time enough to think about the incident and realised that if I had seen the Jaguar literally on my own doorstep the chances were that they had followed me— and in that case it had not been the action of a couple of cheap-thrill seekers. And since I had no known enemies it was evident that the attack had been connected with my visit to Radford. Apparently Heyman had telephoned the shop when I failed to arrive but I had not returned the call, deliberately. Nor did I want to discuss it with the police.

I told Inspector Murdoch of my brief from the ABA but that I'd had no leads to date nor any idea who might be responsible for the attack. I repeated my description of the Jag's two occupants but generally appeared bewildered by the event. The Inspector was no fool and I sensed that he did not altogether accept my air of innocence but, since I had obviously been completely frank in the information I had supplied, he could not be too critical. He probed a little about my enquiries and how they differed from those of the police and I answered honestly, but complicating the issue with technicalities and irrelevant background that might have sounded impressive but gave nothing away. He appeared to let it go at that and then as he stood up to leave, politely refusing a glass of whisky, he seemed to remember a final innocuous question. "Oh . . . by the way, Mr Coll, just so that we don't get our lines crossed . . . you *would* consider it your duty as a citizen to inform the police of any progress in this stolen books business?" he asked with a kindly smile.

"My enquiry is entirely unofficial," I replied. "That means that if we can do anything to track down the people responsible we would be *obliged* to bring in the police."

His smile was less effusive, merely polite. "That's not quite what I meant, sir. I don't need to be reminded you have no powers. What I meant is that you might at some stage, quite inadvertently, be obstructing justice without realising it. Frankly, I don't know what the other police forces are doing about your missing books but it would be stupid to assume they are sitting back and doing nothing . . ."

"There's no suggestion of that . . ." I interrupted

66

tamely but he waved a deprecating hand.

"You may well know more about antiquarian books than we do but you wouldn't contest that we know more about *criminals* than the ABA or any of its representatives?"

I nodded contritely—the only way to deal with the police when on shaky ground—and hoped he would go. But I had underestimated him. He sat down again and stared at me. Reluctantly I returned to my seat. "Something still worrying you, Inspector?" I asked.

"Criminals, Mr Coll. We are talking about criminals," he continued. "People who steal cars and use them for unlawful purposes, as opposed to joy-rides—are criminals."

I nodded, slightly uneasy.

"So, it becomes *my* responsibility."

I smiled. "I don't follow you, Inspector. There's surely no argument. I gave you all the information I have."

He raised his eyebrows and added appreciatively. "Quite detailed. It's apparent you have a trained eye . . ."

"I have a reasonable memory," I conceded.

"That's what I would have thought," he said. "There's nothing secretive about where you were going, Mr Coll?"

My heart sank. "What d'you mean?"

He smiled. "Well, we have to use a lot of discretion in our job—particularly when witnesses fail to come forward for fear of incriminating themselves in some quite irrelevant issue. For example, if you were having a liaison with a married woman I could understand your reluctance . . ."

"What reluctance?"

"To tell us where you were headed this morning?"

I dared not lie. "A college library at Radford. A routine business call. It didn't seem terribly important."

He sighed; it seemed with relief. "Mebbe not. But I thought you would have mentioned it. It's the story Mr Appleton told me earlier but when I asked him if anyone had telephoned the person you were due to meet he told me that the librarian had himself phoned . . . yet, strangely enough, you still haven't returned the call, routine or not . . ?"

"That was remiss of me. Everything has been a whirl since I took that swim," I protested.

He nodded but continued. "You see, when I learnt the car had been stolen I began to scratch around for motives for harming you. Phoning the librarian, Mr Heyman, was an automatic reaction on my part. I enquired why you were meeting and he explained that it was something to do with the robbery they had some months ago."

"That's right," I confirmed.

"But that's not what you told me a few moments ago. And if I wanted to sound melodramatic I might assume that someone wanted to prevent that meeting?"

I was tired of being on the defensive and decided to take the bull by the horns. "You mentioned discretionary powers. I'd like to strike a bargain."

He pulled a face. "Depends. I must tell you now, it is impossible for the police to suppress information or for you to withhold it."

"I'm not withholding evidence but I'm prepared to *volunteer* information, in exchange for something of practical value from you."

"I can't make a deal until I know what's involved," he argued.

"And I'm not prepared to co-operate unless I'm allowed to finish my enquiry."

"I'm not stopping you."

"No, but you can brush me aside if you get the bit between your teeth. I'm convinced that I will have better results if I'm allowed to keep my head start."

He lifted his arms expressively, signalling his helplessness. "I'm prepared to take a gamble but only if you're completely frank with me. If I have any reason to doubt your integrity I'll come down on you like a ton of bricks."

I nodded. "Agreed, in exchange for a piece of information from you. I need Edward Heyman's private address in Lyme Regis. He stays at the college during the week and goes home at weekends and for holidays."

He regarded me with suspicion. "Why do you want that?"

I promised to tell him after I had explained the conclusions drawn from my initial interview with Heyman. He listened quietly. I was completely frank and concluded by asking if he accepted my premise.

"Premise, yes, evidence, no," he said.

"Precisely. That's why I want to have another go at him. We have little enough to go on but I'm scared that if the police question him now, after the fright he's already had, his operation may simply go to ground. Heyman will *know* he's under suspicion. If it's just me his people will think they have nothing to fear."

He laughed. "You must be an optimist. If it *was* them who tried to nobble you this morning they won't be scared to try again."

I shrugged. "The more they show their hand, the more evidence we are likely to collect. We made a start today with the descriptions I gave you."

"I can't complain about that," he agreed. "And since you're a responsible adult I can't stop you sticking your neck out. But why do you want to see Heyman at his home?"

"No special reason—just want to get him away from his library. That's where he's really in his element; where he thinks more clearly."

"You think he's the ringleader?"

I admitted I was uncertain. "I believe he could be obsessional about certain rare books—enough to want to steal them. But he wouldn't know how to break into a doll's house, let alone a strange building at night, and I doubt whether he is ruthless enough to have me killed or maimed . . ."

"More likely a cog in the wheel?"

I nodded. "Probably. He'd certainly have access to information on what was around and where it was located. But quite apart from the physical operation I doubt whether he would know where to fence the stuff, either."

Murdoch snapped incredibly long fingers. "Very well, Mr Coll—you're on," he declared. "We'll concentrate on the criminal aspect and leave you to carry on as before—on the strict understanding that you keep me informed. Watch yourself with Mr Heyman. If he should claim that there was any intimidation or he has been molested in any way I can do nothing for you."

We shook hands on the deal.

Murdoch kept his word in letting me have Heyman's home address. All he had to do was to ask the local police station, who had such information on file in case of fire or robbery, but the point is—he did. I went to look for myself and found a modern apartment block on the perimeter of the town, the sort of place to which City people, accustomed to modern comforts, like to retire. Built in the 1960s, it was set in its own grounds, protected from the road by heavy shrubs.

On Friday evening I had a further tip-off that Heyman had left the college and was presumably driving home. I waited in the grounds in my hired Cortina until he arrived, and after five minutes went up in the lift and rang the bell. He made no effort to conceal his shock at seeing me and before he had time to recover his composure I had brushed past him into the flat.

Despite the Inspector's warning I felt I had little to lose in frightening Heyman; he was a clever man and we might go round in circles indefinitely until my brain was dulled by persistent stonewalling. He'd had ample time to compose a watertight story. Besides, I had been badly frightened; I didn't see why he should escape punishment in kind.

He tried to bridge the gulf between us by asking why I had not been in touch since my "accident" but I ignored the question and pushed past him along the narrow corridor of his flat. "Come in . . ." he said with unintentional humour as I looked about me. The layout was conventional, with rooms on either side of the passageway: first on the left, the bathroom; first right, a small bedroom; second left, the main bedroom; second right, the sitting-room; and at the end of the passage the kitchen. Uninvited, I stuck my head in every room, switching on lights where necessary, while he followed me nervously and without any visible annoyance at my behaviour. When my curiosity had been satisfied I gestured him to precede me into the sitting-room, sparsely furnished in a surprisingly modern style, with the exception of a huge magogany glass-fronted bookcase which, planned or not, dominated the room. I walked over to it and glanced inside at an interesting collection of reference books on early printing and binding. Although not especially valuable as collector's items they were scarce enough to be worth in total about £1000. The value to him would have been much greater.

Reassured by my obvious interest, he asked if I would like a coffee or tea. I turned and stared at him until he looked away. "This is not a social visit, Mr Heyman," I announced. He was standing with the back of his legs against a settee and I added, "Sit down!" He did as I commanded and I moved closer, standing over him menacingly. "You may have wondered why the ABA asked me to conduct this investigation? I'm not a detective . . ." I waited for a response but he looked up at me mutely before shaking his head. "I think I did mention that I'd become a bookseller because I'd had my fill of the nastiness in this world . . . but I never bothered to explain what I actually did. I don't like talking about it but the truth is that I *questioned* people . . ." I smiled encouragingly and he looked terrified.

Heyman started to raise his hand, as though requesting permission to speak or leave the room, and I snapped "Yes?" He pointed unhappily at his pack of cigarettes and asked if he might have one. I refused.

"*Prisoners* under interrogation are denied all privileges," I pointed out, making it sound as though he was totally in my power. "You see, Mr Heyman, when I had all the time in the world I'd quite enjoy a battle of wits. But when I was feeling impatient, for one reason or another, I'd have to resort to unpleasantness. I'm pushed for time now . . ."

My biggest fear was that he would call my bluff, because the prospect of beating him up in cold blood was abhorrent to me, but he capitulated immediately. "They said they only wanted to scare you off," he said appealingly, looking from me to the cigarettes on the table. I handed them to him and he lit one gratefully, gulping in the smoke as though it were oxygen.

"But you were involved in the thefts at Radford?" I said.

He shook his head violently. "It's been a terrible experience. When I arrived on the scene so quickly they were just leaving by the front door—two of them—and we came face to face. They were wearing stocking masks and looked absolutely terrifying. One of them grabbed me by the scuff of the neck and threatened to kill me if I told the police I had seen them. They said they knew where I lived and would come after me. I could see they were deadly serious so I said nothing to the police. A few days later they telephoned to remind me. This time they left a number and said that if anyone made any significant enquiries I was to let them know."

I reached out and took the cigarette from his mouth. He blinked at me tearfully. "You just said they only wanted to scare me," I pointed out irritably, "yet they had already threatened to kill you. What d'you think they were going to do? Invite me to a poetry-reading session?"

He looked longingly at the cigarette in my hand before answering. "The first threat was made in the heat of the moment. They were alarmed at being caught red-handed. The second time, on the phone, they didn't sound quite so bad. I just capitulated. You know what it's like . . . once you give in to blackmail you're hooked for good . . ."

I did not comment but asked for the telephone number he had been given. He shrugged. "I threw it away."

I stubbed out the cigarette in an ash tray, walked back to the bookcase and opened the glass doors. "How many years did it take you to collect this lot—or were they stolen?" I asked, knowing they probably represented a lifetime's loving work. He was too apprehensive to answer and watched, fascinated, as I ran my fingers along the rows of books until I had selected one, finely bound in light brown calf and cleverly decorated in gilt. I removed it and took it over to him. As he reached out to retrieve the book I withdrew it tantalisingly. "You're not being frank with me, Mr Heyman," I announced. "I shall have to demonstrate the more unpleasant side to my nature."

"Don't do anything to these books," he croaked appealingly.

"I had a soaking in the river this week, thanks to you. If I gave you a taste of your own medicine you'd probably drown—and that would be murder. But if your *books* were to be lost in the river . . ?"

"You wouldn't . . !"

I regarded him with contempt. "I want that telephone number."

He stared at the calf-bound book and back at me and suddenly called my bluff. "You'd rather throw *me* in the river than those books. You're a bibliophile too. You couldn't do that."

I had no alternative but to shatter that conviction. I instructed him to follow me into the kitchen, where I dropped the book into the sink and turned on the tap. My conscience made me ensure that the jet of water did not actually strike the book, but it was quickly covered in a fine spray. Heyman dived for the tap but I held him at a distance until he capitulated.

"01 930 3274," he called out.

I let him get to the book and dry it tenderly with a towel, before leading him back to the sitting-room, where I made a note of the number. Then I dialled the number and handed him the receiver. "Tell them I'm here now," I instructed.

Cowed, he looked away and waited as the bell rang at the other end. After a few minutes it was evident that there would be no reply. I made him replace the receiver and commented, "That was very convenient for you. Now I haven't any way of knowing whether or not you were lying." He kept his eyes averted and said nothing.

Assuring him I would try later, I asked what guarantee I had that he would not try to warn them when I had gone. He swore that he was finished with the crooks and was relieved to have unburdened his conscience at last. I was tempted to believe him but not prepared to take any more chances. Besides, I had not yet mentioned his response to the "bait" paragraph in the newsletter. It was not an enquiry that could have been made under coercion and in any case the newsletter would have been sent to him. Either he had rung of his own accord or he had told someone else who had made him check. I decided to keep this extra card up my sleeve. Instead I put on something of an act to convince him I had swallowed his story. I conceded that his predicament must have been a nightmare; now that he had taken a new stand I was prepared to call on his assistance at some later stage to help "nail" the thieves. The net was surely closing in, I assured him.

He nodded eagerly although keeping an apprehensive eye on me as he reached out for the cigarettes with mounting confidence. This time I did not impede him and stood up to leave. He started to rise but I waved him back. "I can show myself out," I said and looked at him with what I hoped passed for sincerity. "I really *can* trust you, can't I?"

As I may have mentioned earlier he did not have an expressive face but he seemed to try very hard to convey the desire to make amends. "I've been a fool," he admitted, the normal monotone delivered with greater emphasis to illustrate his new-found integrity.

He started to rise again but I stared down at him. "I said I would show myself out."

Heyman smiled nervously but stayed where he was as I left the room and turned along the short passage. I made a show of opening the front door, called out again and waited for a response before slamming the door. Silently I doubled back to the nearest bedroom where I hid behind the door. After a couple of minutes Heyman came out of the sitting-room and carefully opened the front door, listening for the sound of the lift or footsteps on the stairs. When he heard neither he must have assumed I had already gone. He closed the front door and returned—this time, I imagined, to look out of the sitting-room window. I crept out of the bedroom and waited outside, looking through the crack in the open door and dodging back as he returned to the coffee-table to pick up the telephone. By listening to the sounds of him dialling I could tell it did not have the long-distance London 01 prefix he had given me, and guessed it was a local call. Frustratingly, he did not ask for anyone by name, merely announcing himself and asking to be put through.

When his contact eventually answered Heyman sighed noisily. "I've just about had enough . . . That's all very well but you're not involved . . . It's that special investigator from the ABA, Matthew Coll—that ducking in the river had the opposite effect to the one intended by those . . . those barbarians . . . No, he didn't phone, just turned up here out of the blue. Frightened the life out of me . . . He's a nasty piece of work . . . No, I didn't say anything . . . no, nothing at all. Don't you trust me? What's that? . . . Naturally . . . well, I had to say something so I gave him a cock-and-bull story about being intimidated. Now he thinks I'm on his side . . . Of course I didn't say who they were—which is true because I don't even know myself! He asked for a telephone number and I gave him one of the London reference libraries, so he can't get a reply until Monday. Perhaps we can think of something else by then . . . No, that won't do. Don't underestimate him . . . I don't think *anyone* should do *anything* for some time . . . especially not me. I'm the only lead he has . . . Yes, thanks . . . yes, I knew you would understand . . . Will I see you next week? Good . . . good-bye then."

He put the phone down and when I walked in the whole of his upper body jumped with fright. His mute alarm was satisfying and I smiled, saying nothing to heighten the suspense. Eventually he could stand it no longer and tried to explain that the phone call had not been what I probably imagined. I shook my head disbelievingly and he fell silent. I wanted to hurt him but still hesitated over striking him in cold blood, especially the first blow. Heyman was not only undersized but so out of condition it would have been like beating a child. I searched for some way of humiliating him, as he cowered pathetically, and I eventually sat down beside him, reached out and took hold of his bony nose. I squeezed, bringing tears to his eyes, and he yelled for mercy, complaining that he could not breathe. His mouth was opening and closing like a fish and I decided to take him at his word. I clamped my other hand over his mouth, pulled his head back against my chest and forced his jaws shut. Now it was impossible for him to breathe and he panicked, eyes popping and arms flailing, but I could control his movements with little effort. After a minute or so he was about to pass out and I released him. He gasped despairingly for air, his tear-stained face red and swollen, his wizened chest heaving painfully. I slowly extended my hand again in the direction of his nose and he shrank back terrified.

"Please, I'll tell you anything."

"I believed you before but you lied . . ."

He shook his head exhaustedly. "I'm not cut out for this sort of thing."

I took the telephone receiver and unscrewed the ear and mouthpieces. Then I smashed the delicate mechanism at each end in the fireplace. "That'll stop a repeat performance when I've gone," I told him.

He ignored the damaged phone. "I'm beaten anyway. There's no-one to ring."

"We'll start again then. First, you *did* rob your own library?"

He nodded.

"The alarm was set off merely to make it look like an outside job?"

He nodded again.

"What happened to the books?"

"I've got one hidden away—my favourite. The others have probably been sold by now . . ."

77

"You don't know?"

He did not answer, replying with a question of his own. "If I managed to get all the books back do you think I might escape being arrested?"

I shrugged. "That's not for me to say. There isn't just the Radford job to consider."

"I don't know anything about the others."

"But you acted as an adviser?"

He studied me shrewdly, surprised at my apparent knowledge and nodded reluctantly. "I swear I don't know the people. They contacted me and I've never dared enquire about their identity.

Having heard him on the phone I was inclined to believe that part of his story. "OK, we'll leave that for now. But who was that on the phone just now?"

"Believe me, that was just a friend to whom I turned for advice. She had nothing to do with all this."

"She?"

He shook his head. "She's not involved."

I reached for his nose again and he disintegrated. "I'll tell you . . . but it won't help. She's totally innocent. It's Lady Berridge."

I was stunned. "Caroline Berridge?" I queried.

He nodded.

FIVE

My satisfaction at having linked Heyman with the robberies was dampened by his disclosure that Caroline Berridge was (at the very least, it seemed) a confidante. He had, admittedly, insisted that she knew nothing of his involvement. Indeed under further pressure he had elaborated on the unlikely relationship; recollecting the manner in which it had developed from common interest in books. Initially his contribution had been the offer of professional advice but in return her intelligence and receptiveness had gradually become a sounding-board for his dreams and ideas. She was soon a friend to whom he could talk uninhibitedly, to confide the seldom appreciated stresses and strains of his work as a college librarian. An unattractive man in most senses of the word, he readily conceded that he had no friends outside the cloistered library world.

True, he had deceived me before, but I could not believe Lady Berridge was anything more than what he now maintained. Despite the strong sexual attraction that might have clouded the judgement of other men I felt I was able to judge her with reasonable detachment. Under the most clinical appraisal she still came over to me as a person of integrity. Caroline Berridge was obviously no wilting wallflower. Despite that delicate appearance and her gentle manner there was an underlying resilience. I could visualise her leaving no stone unturned to protect the welfare of her husband and the Berridge estates. But people like Caroline seemed to follow a code that ruled out-of-court activities that might compromise 'honour' and the family's good name.

Much as I hated to admit it even to myself, the mere thought of seeing her again was stimulating and the awareness of this vulnerability was a surprisingly humiliating sensation. I had assumed, having complacently dismissed her from my thoughts after the first meeting, when that shining new Aston Martin had brought me down to earth, that I could look on her as any other attractive married woman with whom I had routine business dealings. And if our paths had not been crossing again so soon I would have taken the situation in my stride. But I knew that I could not ignore Heyman's telephone call and that I would have to see her again to check him out conclusively. Although I could not believe there was any dishonest association I was all *too* aware that Heyman had lied before. It was probably safer to proceed on the assumption that he had lied again.

I toyed with the idea of driving straight from Heyman's flat to Oldham Park but hesitated—partly, I told myself, because I did not want to risk embarrassing her in front of Lord Berridge. More accurately, because I wanted to see her alone. It was a measure of my anxiety that I managed somehow to justify the double assumption that by arriving unannounced I might catch her off-guard—if indeed she had something to hide— and that it would be more productive to see her alone, where I could study her reactions without distractions. Anticipating that on a Saturday afternoon Lord Berridge might be out, probably shooting on the estate, I drove over next day, leaving the shop in the hands of Charlie Appleton.

I was out of luck. I should have realised that running a stately home is not a simple five-day week job. While Lord Berridge was predictably out the housekeeper, a smartly dressed woman in her mid-forties, looking more like a companion than a servant, informed me that Caroline was "in conference" and could not be disturbed. I asked if I could wait. The woman took me into the library and returned a few minutes later with the message that I was welcome to make myself comfortable and that Lady Berridge would "collect" me within twenty minutes. Ironically, I'm not the most patient of men when it comes to waiting but my reaction now to the short time-span was one of mild irritation. In a blissful setting like this I knew I would be completely oblivious of time.

I looked about me; the problem was *where* to start. So I did the logical thing, turned left at the door and started to work my way round systematically, using the step-ladder to ensure that I did not miss the levels outside one's immediate vision. I stopped at authors and titles that interested me, examining the copies carefully and, setting myself the challenge of trying to put a price on them; relating such factors as condition and the quality of binding and print to age and rarity. I had no check-list against which to compare my educated guesses but it was an amusing pastime.

The books were arranged alphabetically and under section B my gaze was attracted to a cluster of early editions of John Bunyan, the man who gave us *Pilgrim's Progress*. As I perused the different titles and wondered which to bring down my mouth suddenly went dry and I became conscious of a peculiar contraction at my throat. *The Life and Death of Mr Badman* was surely one of the stolen books? I found Frensham's list in my inside breast pocket and compared notes. Under the same title I read: ". . . dark brown morocco, gilt titling on spine . . ." I looked up and saw that the description tallied. Now, if it was the same 1680 edition I was faced with a major problem of diplomacy. I could scarcely justify appearing at Oldham Park uninvited and in my opening gambit come out with a less than friendly remark like . . . "I have reason to believe (which is hardly my style to start with) . . . that you are in possession of stolen property . . ."

My hands had started to perspire and instinctively I wiped the palms on my trousers rather than risk marking the leather binding. I took the book down and opened it at the title page. The first blob of print that I focussed on was the date: 1680. Surely this *must* be the missing book? It had to be more than a coincidence. I turned back to the first endpaper where, facing, I saw the bold Berridge bookplate—a Charles II galleon with the family coat of arms entwined with the rigging, a reference presumably to the origins of the Berridge family fortune. I took the book over to the window and tried to examine the bookplate to see if it might have been added recently or whether it might have concealed another marking but I was not skilled enough to tell. It didn't *look* suspicious.

I glanced back at the sea of books—so many that from a distance they resembled undulating strips of polished leather—and it occurred to me that one could not find a more suitable hiding-place for stolen books than among other similar books! Irritably I demolished the theory. What possible motive could Caroline have for concealing stolen books? Money? I tried to dismiss the suggestion but it nagged at my subconscious. The doubts switched to Lord Berridge but under close scrutiny they seemed even more unlikely. Berridge's shortcomings were probably related to his limited horizons. He was a fool perhaps but not a criminal. Caroline was certainly no fool but I could not imagine her selling that integrity for money.

What did I do now? If I insisted on continuing the search systematically would I be asked to leave? Was I making a fool of myself? After all, there might be several copies in existence of most of the titles on my list of missing books. I wondered what Wilfred Frensham would do. But then I pulled myself together and stopped prevaricating. I would simply stop browsing for fun and concentrate instead of looking for titles on my list. Before long I came across a second 'coincidence', a rare topographical item: Paterson (Lieut. W), *A Narrative of the four journeys into the country of Hottentots and Caffrania, 1789*. The condition of both was similar but again the copy in my possession bore the reassuring Berridge bookplate.

The 'suspect' book was still open in my hands when Caroline Berridge joined me. I was so preoccupied that the anticipated excitement was missing and when she apologised for keeping me waiting I glanced at my watch and realised that forty minutes had elapsed. I made an effort to appear relaxed. "Please don't apologise. I told you last time—being left in here is no imposition. Quite the reverse."

Even as the words tumbled out the power of her attraction began to assert itself. Dressed in a simple but obviously expensive cashmere twin-set—the style I imagine she favoured since the outfit was similar to the one she had worn the last time we had met—she looked stunningly beautiful, in the traditional English way. The colours were pastel, delicate and soft, and there was an ethereal quality about the picture, about her features and her elegance, that set her apart from other women. I tried to strike a balance by thinking of Laura but her most attractive features, the vividness and that scintillating personality, suddenly seemed quite brash and overwhelming in comparison. It was probably the air of tranquility, the poise, that entranced me. Although she seemed to have hurried to greet me, genuinely concerned at her neglect, the manner was so composed considerations of Time were put in perspective and that meant of little importance.

Caroline smiled and my heart took flight again. "I guessed as much," she replied happily. "I must admit that was the reason I didn't try to break off the meeting any earlier." She suddenly noticed the volume in my hand. "What is that you're hugging so possessively? It's not for sale!"

I remembered why I was here and announced in what I hoped was an even, matter-of-fact voice: "It seems to have been stolen. At least, it's one of the titles on my list."

Her eyes switched from the book to me curiously but I kept my face expressionless. Eventually she laughed and replied: "I'm a little slow on the uptake at times. I thought you were serious for a moment."

I closed the covers and held the book out to her. "I *was* serious, insofar as its on my list. See for yourself . . ." I also passed her the typewritten sheet.

Caroline ignored it and looked at me intently. "And *you* think that *this* is the stolen copy?"

She was hurt and I was on dangerous ground. I hesitated. "No . . . I didn't say that. When you walked in I was merely marvelling at the coincidence."

She was far from mollified. "Surely not once you saw the bookplate? We have an impressive collection, as you can see, and it is inevitable you would find copies of highly desirable titles . . . *several* of which you might find on any list of stolen items. I wouldn't really have been surprised if you had found half-a-dozen among the many thousands of rare books you can see there."

"I did find one another," I conceded, drawing her attention to the Bunyan. "It's my job, at least in the circumstances, to be aware of coincidences—even if there's nothing to it."

"Even?" she protested gently.

"I'm sorry, Caroline. I didn't mean to be offensive."

She replaced the Paterson with the calm authority of the librarian who knows where things go. "I'm not offended but just the same I'll unearth the original documentation or the sales invoices, if we have them."

I flushed, humbled by her sincerity. "That won't be necessary, really."

She was adamant. "I'm not overreacting. But I value my friendships. I wouldn't want the rapport we seem to have to be eroded by even the slightest suspicion. I couldn't bear it."

I was humiliated and shrugged helplessly. "What can I say to apologise?"

She smiled. "Nothing. You were just doing your job. Come and have some tea . . . I'd like you to meet someone." She turned to lead the way to the family's private drawing-room and I followed, relieved that I had been forgiven but quietly disappointed that we would not be alone.

"I've been meeting this afternoon with Billy Lloyd," she explained as we took a diversion to avoid the area reserved for visitors. "You may have heard of him . . . the new rising force in the City. The papers are full of Billy and his wheeling and dealing. He's a friend of Henry's and mine and we're lucky enough to have him as a partner in a special promotion we're running at Oldham Park next month. He's an absolute genius for business of any sort, more particularly for making money, and he's been a godsend to us in running this mausoleum."

I was not over-enthusiastic at the prospect of meeting the apparent gift from Heaven she seemed to admire so much, no matter how sanctimoniously boring he undoubtedly was. I had an aversion to City types and his being a friend of the toffee-nosed Lord Berridge was no recommendation. I had a shock in store. The man rising from an armchair to greet me was in his early thirties, perhaps even a year or two younger than me. I had not reckoned on his physical attraction either. An inch or so shorter than my six feet, he was powerfully built in a healthy bullish way and his features were pleasant and even. Scar tissue over his right eyebrow and a slight thickening of an otherwise straight nose seemed slightly incongruous perhaps and when he smiled I was conscious of the exceptional evenness of the teeth in his lower jaw. False, perhaps. He might well have lost his own teeth and inherited those marks from one of the so-called 'contact' sports—rugby or boxing, perhaps.

His good looks were suddenly familiar and I realised I had seen that face before. My sluggish memory cells responded at last and I recognised him, at the same time as remembering his name, as a popular light heavyweight boxer, a British champion if I was right, who had retired to make even more money as a businessman. Now it all began to fit into place. The sober pinstripe three-piece suit was too stylish and distinctive for the City one associates with stockbrokers and bankers. Lloyd had made his money initially in restaurants and boutiques before moving into property and commercial banking.

He looked what he was—successful and still ambitious—and when he grasped my hand and introduced himself simply: "Lloyd . . . Billy. Pleased to meet you," I sensed I was in the company of someone special, a winner. I liked him instinctively despite my awareness of the apparent intimacy between him and Caroline. I introduced myself and after Caroline had used the internal phone to order tea she told him: "Matthew runs an antiquarian bookshop at Ardley, just a few miles away."

"Really? How interesting . . ." Lloyd replied, with what I assumed was a platitude, although I was to be surprised for a second time. "You don't match the image I have of booksellers," he added.

From someone else that remark might have sounded offensive but the directness of his gaze indicated that he was merely speaking his mind. I tried to place his slight accent and thought I detected faint Cockney origins.

I smiled politely. "Assuming that the picture you have of the trade is fairly standard, what *do* I look like then?"

He returned the smile mechanically; his eyes indifferent. "I'm interested in people and their behaviour patterns but I haven't had an opportunity to observe you for long enough. I'd be restricted to mannerisms, which are not as reliable. Fascinating subject. Someone once wrote a book on it . . ."

"Aren't you ducking the issue?" I challenged.

He studied me closely for a minute, opened his mouth to speak and was interrupted by the arrival of tea on a trolley, giving him a further opportunity to watch me. When Caroline broke in to pour the tea and offer us toast and cakes his eyes never left my face. Eventually, when the housekeeper had left, leaving the trolley, he began again: "My immediate impression is one of awareness . . . *alertness* might be a better word. A man of action, not someone to be confined by the four walls of a little country bookshop . . ."

I nodded encouragingly. "Maybe, but as you can see I'm not exactly imprisoned by the shop. With respect, Mr Lloyd, you're still ducking out . . ."

"Billy," he corrected. "Then, with *respect*, Matthew . . ."

"Matt," I corrected.

"Matt," he echoed, "I'd say you looked like a policeman."

I smiled but inwardly bristled. I didn't feel like a policeman and resented his intuition. At the same moment I decided that I resented his composure, his politeness but obvious indifference to me and . . . the equally apparent bond between him and Caroline. I had envied Frensham's composure but his manner had been rather different; that of an older man towards someone of considerably less experience in a shared profession; but he had made it clear he respected me for the specialist talents he did not possess. Billy Lloyd had the single-mindedness of a young man on his way to the top, not terribly concerned about whose toes he stepped on

87

getting there. I wondered what my reaction might have been had positions been reversed and I had been asked to guess his occupation. "Too good to be true" might have been the instinctive reaction although no doubt I would not have been discourteous enough to voice that sentiment. He did look too good to be true, a good-looking actor, a Robert Redford playing a role or a personality 'manufactured' by the persuasion industry.

Caroline was looking at me expectantly and I forced myself to sound pleasant and intrigued at his assessment. "Impressive," I conceded. "That's exactly what I am—or trying to be."

Caroline smiled reassuringly, as though she realised I was being polite for her sake. "Matt is being modest," she interjected. "He is rather special. The antiquarian book trade has suffered a series of thefts of rather valuable books from libraries and the more important bookshops. The police obviously don't really know where to start, so Matt was called in by the bigwigs in the trade as an expert investigator."

Normally I'm repelled by flattery but Caroline was so obviously impressed by my appointment that I was quite childishly pleased at the build-up. "Like Sherlock Holmes," I countered to lighten the mood and he smiled.

A hint of fresh respect appeared in his expression. "You mean that your knowledge of these books could be useful in identifying the sort of people who might be involved and where to find the stuff?"

I nodded. "Something like that. I used to be in military intelligence, which also helps."

He grinned. "So I *was* right!" The businessman in him came to the surface. "You must get good money . . . as a consultant?"

I didn't know how to answer but Caroline came to my aid. "All Bill ever thinks about is money—perhaps that's why he's so rich . . ."

Lloyd reacted indignantly. "Who says I'm rich? I'm not, in the usual sense. Successful, perhaps, but I started with nothing so I had a long way to catch up. Besides, what *is* rich? One million, two, a hundred . . ?"

He looked from Caroline to me and I shrugged. "It depends on who one asks. Stately home owner, bookseller or entrepreneur. We'd all have different answers."

Caroline interjected. "Mine would probably surprise you. For stately home read 'millstone'. I don't know how Henry and I would manage if it wasn't for the help and advice of people like Bill."

Lloyd munched his toast as though he had barely heard. She poured me another cup of tea and as she passed it to me our hands touched. I felt a current of excitement and I looked up instinctively, my guard momentarily down. As our eyes met she smiled warmly and it was an effort not to look away. Was there something more than friendship there? Or was my imagination making a fool of me. Was she conscious too of a special empathy or was she merely a warm-hearted person who responded to all her friends in this fashion? There was undoubtedly a relaxed intimacy between her and Lloyd but that was surely understandable in view of the help he was giving her husband.

She glanced up at the imposing grandfather clock near the fireplace and then back at me. "Henry should be back within the next half-an-hour. You will stay to see him, Matt?"

I looked unconsciously at my watch, without really noticing what the hands read, and suddenly remembered why I had come. The discovery in the library had confused the issue and the subsequent preoccupation with Lloyd had jostled aside the memory of Heyman's confession and his mysterious telephone call.

"Actually I won't stay but perhaps I could have two

89

minutes of your time before I go . . ?"

Her eyes widened with concern. "Oh Matt, please forgive me. It didn't occur to me that this wasn't just a social call. How presumptuous of me!"

I was assailed by another wave of embarrassment at what would inevitably seem to her like an underhand approach. "It's nothing important. I was reasonably near, so I thought I'd pop in and just check something out."

"Of course. Don't let's waste any more of your time . . ." she insisted.

I was uncomfortably aware of Lloyd's presence. I looked at him and he returned my stare with amusement before heaving himself out of the armchair and announcing that he would just stretch his legs.

Caroline told him to sit down and that "we" had no secrets but to his credit he shrugged off the protestation and left. When the door had closed behind him Caroline rounded on me worriedly. "Matt, that was embarrassing. We can't afford to alienate Mr Lloyd—we need him far more than he needs us."

I shrugged. "He *volunteered* to leave. I said nothing to embarrass him—he simply did the gentlemanly thing. Besides, in all fairness, what I had to say is of no concern of his . . ."

"We don't have any secrets. He knows as much about Oldham Park as our accountant or the lawyer—probably more. Henry places great store by his advice."

I nodded appreciatively. "I've no doubt . . . although since you mentioned a business partnership, a promotion of some sort, presumably he gets something in return?" As I voiced my thoughts I was conscious of an element of cynicism in the question, jealousy perhaps, but Caroline did not notice and her response was serious.

"Relatively nothing. I don't know why he bothers. Without being unkind, perhaps it's a degree of snobbishness, mixing with the so-called aristocracy. Henry and his family are rather upper-crust, you know, and Billy's circumstances were rather humble. But they genuinely get on very well together—they have this interest in shooting . . . spend hours fussing over guns of one sort or another . . ."

I hesitated before asking her what was uppermost in my mind and tried to phrase it innocuously, with a laugh. "It's pretty obvious he's fond of you. It's nice to see the age of chivalry is not dead."

But this time she saw through me and she touched my hand lightly. Her expression was amused but not mocking. "Matthew Coll. I do believe you're jealous . . ?"

I was forced to meet her halfway with a self-conscious laugh and an admission. "Of course. I wouldn't deny it."

She squeezed my hand. "Bless you. It does wonders for a woman's ego to know that a man she admires finds her attractive. I can set your mind at rest about Billy. He's a darling and I do like him very much.

"I'm not a snob, believe me, but we come from different worlds. He's a talented and warm-hearted person but a bit of a rough diamond and while that should make no difference to a man like Henry who can appreciate manly qualities I need to *communicate* . . . with people who talk the same language, have an interest in the things that are important to me . . . literature and the arts."

Reassured, I smiled at her. "Remind me to show you my etchings one of these days."

Her eyes went down to her hand still trapped in mine but she made no attempt to withdraw. "Matt, would you be upset if I asked you not to come too often? It's just that we have perhaps too much in common . . . we could be such friends but . . ."

"But what?" I nequired anxiously.

91

"But would it stop at that? You must realise that I'm very attracted to you. To keep on seeing you would only create problems."

My heart had leapt with delight at the unexpected confession. Nothing else seemed to matter by comparison with this devastating news. The thought of losing her now, knowing that she shared my feelings, was painful but I sensed there was little I could do to make her change her mind. Tamely I suggested that we should leave the future to take care of itself.

She shook her head and gently withdrew her hand. "No, Matt. I believe we control our own destinies. I have a strong sense of duty and could never betray my husband, no matter how much I ever loved another man. I regard the marriage vows as sacred, corny though that might seem, and if I must suffer as a consequence, then so be it. Can you understand that?"

If anything, my respect for her soared to new heights and I was unable to answer. I nodded dumbly. Caroline smiled sadly, moved back to put a few feet between us and took a deep breath before adding: "Please let's change the subject. What is it you wanted to ask me?"

It took several seconds for me to adjust to the change in mood and subconsciously I gave myself a vigorous shake. Only then was I able to tell her about my fake paragraph in the Library Association's newsletter. "We were really setting bait in the hope that we could attract interest from someone with less than honest motives," I explained. "One of the enquiries—and we're following them all up—happened to be from Mr Heyman at Radford College and since that was the site of one of the robberies I was understandably suspicious."

She struggled to control her indignation. "That's perfectly ridiculous, Matt. Obviously you don't know him. He's a *delightful* man."

"I'm sure he is, but most of us tend to make excuses for those we like, make allowances when in other cases we would be quite intolerant. But I've spoken to Heyman and I must admit I'm not entirely satisfied."

"Matt, you're suspicious by nature. Only a short while ago you were practically accusing *me* of concealing stolen books."

"Point taken," I concurred, "but no-one is condemned on suspicion alone. You may well be right but just tell me *why* you're so sure—and don't just say he's so nice."

She shrugged. "I told you before, I'm quite shameless in making use of people's specialist knowledge and Mr Heyman has been my principal advisor since I took an interest in the Berridge library. He does it because he loves *books*. Antiquarian books are the only things that really matter in his life."

I nodded. "I accept that, although you've just inadvertently given him a motive. You regard him as a friend . . ?"

"Yes."

"To the extent that he might confide in you?"

"In certain matters I hope so."

"And he's said nothing about any pressures?"

"What sort of pressures? We all have our crosses to bear."

"Such as needing money . . . being blackmailed . . . anything out of the ordinary?" When she shook her head I added cautiously, "Has he mentioned me?"

Caroline reflected for a moment. "Come to think of it, we did compare notes about you—which was a pretty natural reaction for both of us, being at the heart of an investigation. I probably started it. I was interested in you . . . as a person, and like a silly woman I wanted to get his impression . . ."

"And . . ."

She laughed. "He didn't experience quite the same emotion if that's what you mean! But I think he quite liked you . . . thought you'd do a good job."

"Why did he say that?"

She furrowed her brow. "Oh Matt, must you be so persistent? I don't know. I'm just reporting an impression."

I had come to a crossroads. To plunge straight ahead meant relating my interrogation of Heyman and asking her point-blank whose memory was at fault or, more bluntly, which of them was lying. But I did not believe in disclosing my hand prematurely.

Instead I played for safety and took the diversion; shrugging the issue off and telling her to forget it. "Perhaps it would be better if I did stay away for a week or two, at least until we've got to the bottom of this business," I said. "If there's anything you should know I'll phone."

She smiled. "Thank you, Matt, for being so understanding. There's no point in inviting temptation." She opened the door and led the way to the private side entrance. Rather more quickly than I liked she bid me good-bye in a friendly but rather formal manner and the door was closed in my face.

I walked to the end of the drive where the Citroen had been left and, on reaching it, I was suddenly conscious of Billy Lloyd just round the corner. He was in the act of closing and locking the driver's door of the Aston Martin I had noticed on the previous occasion. This time I was able to take in the number plate: BL1. So his visits were obviously not limited to weekends. Lloyd looked up and walked over. "Going now?" he said, somewhat obviously, but his tone was friendly.

I nodded.

He grinned. "Can't get over you being a bookseller . . . Any money in old books?"

I shook my head. "Only when you steal them."

SIX

Monday mornings in the shop are invariably very quiet but since I was not paying Charlie Appleton I had him come in to help in the preparation of a catalogue. I had for some time thought about building a list of mail-order customers, people who might initially buy by post but come down to visit me when they were in this part of the country. Mail-order is a useful adjunct to any bookshop business if one can find the time and many of my colleagues had regular visits from even overseas customers who seemed to search for any excuse to come browsing.

Because he was our first customer that morning I suppose I must have paid special attention to the middle-aged stranger who walked in, nodded casually to both of us and immediately began studying the history section. He was a moon-faced man with a huge domed forehead and pebble-shaped steel-rimmed spectacles which accentuated the roundness; not fat but rotund. He was wearing a dark suit, stiff white collar and tie which more than anything else made him look like a professional man. That in itself might not sound especially noteworthy, except that most of our customers usually dressed casually, weekend browsers from the surrounding towns as well as the regulars. Distinctly formal clothes on a Monday morning somehow seemed out of place unless the man was a doctor on his rounds or a lawyer en route for a court at one of the major towns, which seemed equally remote. Yet he was obviously a bibliophile, browsing single-mindedly and putting aside the copies he presumably intended to buy.

As a matter of courtesy when we had our morning

coffee Charlie offered the stranger a cup and that one gesture apparently converted a casual browser into a potential customer for life. His eyes lit up and he began to chat uninhibitedly in an affected public school accent although his enthusiasm appeared natural enough. Showering us with compliments of the sort we had come to expect of visitors, he asked if we had any other stock not on display and when I showed him the bookroom at the back he was overwhelmed at the sight. Insisting on introducing himself—he said his name was Goodman and that he was a senior partner in a London firm of accountants—he bombarded me with questions about the shop, its turnover and buying and selling patterns and even about my future plans. In other circumstances I might have dealt with such questions abruptly but his enthusiasm was infectious and, assuming he had similar plans of his own, I responded indulgently, answering certain questions and deflecting others. A veil was kept over most of the financial information because at the back of my mind was the faintest suspicion that he might even be an income tax inspector.

Eventually, apparently unaware of my reserve, he seemed to reach an important decision. "You must have been wondering why some of my questions have seemed so indiscreet. You may even have thought I was just plain nosey," he began, inadvertently hitting the nail on the head but not waiting for a confirmation. "I'll tell you. I've been a bibliophile all my life, at least for the past thirty years. Can I talk with you privately?"

He looked from me rather pointedly to Charlie. I shrugged and suggested he could feel free to speak his mind. He sighed, it seemed with relief that he had reached first base. "Then I'll put my cards on the table, Mr Coll. I've been intending to do something about it for years. Always vaguely thought in terms of having a shop when I retired but never done anything about it . . . perhaps because I don't . . . actually retire, that is

96

. . . for another year or so . . . although I'm my own boss. I can retire when I like."

His long-winded prattling was beginning to irritate me and I could see Charlie masking a grin with a hand. I decided to give him a few moments' grace before pleading an urgent appointment and was in the process of switching off my attention when he finally came to the point . . .

"But this morning I fell in love with your shop . . . fell in love," he repeated with an almost pathetic expression. "I want to buy it."

I smiled. "Thank you for the sentiments, Mr Goodman, although you won't be surprised to learn that you're not the first to react in that way. It is a beautiful shop, in a beautiful setting. That's why *I* love it and why it's not for sale."

He smiled anfiously. "Forgive me, I'm not being very businesslike. What I *meant* to say is that I didn't expect the shop to be for sale and therefore I'm prepared to pay considerably more than the market price . . ."

I shrugged. "It's not for sale—period."

Goodman looked from me to Charlie, who turned away and pointedly gave his attention to a pile of books on the floor, and then back to me again. He sniggered a trifle hysterically. "I'm being very unprofessional. As an accountant it goes against the grain to negotiate under duress . . ."

"What duress?" I enquired curiously.

"Infatuation, then. Like a middle-aged man making a fool of himself over a beautiful young girl," he explained. "Making it so obvious to everyone that he's thrown common sense to the winds."

I felt a glimmer of sympathy. "Aren't we all a little irrational at times?" I didn't expect an answer; nor did I expect him to carry on. I was wrong.

Goodman smiled. "Irrational or not, I have one thing

in my favour—whether we're talking about young girls or shops—and that's *money*. Everyone has his or her price."

My hackles rose. "Not me!" I replied aggressively.

Matching my mood he suddenly became more businesslike; there was an imperceptible straightening of his shoulders. "*Everyone*, Mr Coll. If I was to offer a million pounds you'd accept. And once the principle is agreed it should only be a matter of negotiating a price."

I laughed at the patronising assumption. "You make me sound like a high class call-girl but I'll give you the benefit of the doubt. Leaving aside flights of fancy, if you offered me £150,000 my answer would be the same—no."

Goodman's jaw set with determination and his eyes seemed to narrow to mere slits behind the lens of his spectacles. From being an amiable, slightly fussy-looking man he suddenly had an air of menace. "You think I'm just a load of hot air," he said, "and you're trying to call what you imagine is a bluff. But I'll call yours. £150,000 is ridiculous, as you well know, but I will make an offer of £100,000—which is considerably over the odds. You're a young man, Mr Coll—think what you could do with that sort of money."

I saw Charlie's jaw drop and his bewilderment shattered my complacency. I'd had no intention of trying to strike a bargain and I had never even contemplated selling—but then I had never thought in terms of this sort of money. I was being offered a net profit of about £50,000 and the chances were that as an accountant Goodman knew enough dodges to ensure that I did not have to pay capital gains tax. Logic rebelled at the sentiment that kept me chained to Ardley.

It's a chance of a lifetime, you romantic fool, it asserted.

Rubbish—it's too good to be true, you materialistic sod, Coll, I answered myself.

Coll . . . Mr Coll . . . How did Goodman know my name? I made a point of not identifying myself to casual shoppers, preferring them to relate to the shop and not me as an individual; a policy already justified in recent absences when Charlie had been in charge. Customers tend to identify with personalities and sometimes will not even stay if that person is not there. I was positive now that we had not exchanged names when he had introduced himself, nor was there any evidence on the sign outside. Why too had he assumed I was the owner when Charlie probably looked the part, certainly more than me . . ?

I put the point to Goodman as casually as I could and caught him momentarily off-balance. He hesitated before remembering that the shop and my name had been recommended to him by a friend. He mentioned the name but it meant nothing to me.

"Have you just driven down from London?" I asked, hazarding a guess.

He frowned. "Not especially. I was passing through the area and thought it was worth making a small detour to do some browsing." He held up five books he had selected. "You can see it *was* well worth it. I'd like to buy these—but if you'll throw in the shop too my day will have been made . . . and not just this day."

Charlie was staring us openly, apparently dumb-founded by the turn of events. Goodman's expression indicated he thought he had taken the wind out of our sails but the underlying tone of triumph confirmed my decision—the offer *was* too good to be true. With an effort I clung to my politeness. "We'll take your money for the books," I offered, "but not for the shop. Thanks anyway."

His affability evaporated and he studied me closely before answering. "Don't commit yourself now—sleep on it. I'll ring tomorrow, Mr Coll."

I shook my head in a way that demonstrated plainly

he was wasting his time and reached for the books. Goodman pursed his lips angrily and put the books down. "I've changed my mind. Forget it!" Without another word he turned and left.

As the door slammed Charlie finally recovered his voice. "Well I'm damned! What a nutcase!"

I nodded absent-mindedly. But the man's behaviour suggested frustration, not instability, and the apparent contradictions in his story coupled with the circumstances of his visit were suspicious enough to have me thinking along different lines. It had to be more than a coincidence, someone's wanting so desperately to buy the shop *now* and not being prepared to leave a bid in for the future—in a year's time, for example, when he had originally planned to retire; or even think in terms of a partnership whereby his involvement could be more gradual. Why the impatience?

"I take my hat off to you, Matt," announced Charlie with an awed expression. "You'll make a bookseller yet!"

"Oh, why is that?"

He grinned. "Anyone who does this for a living has to be a little short on the old grey matter. And anyone who can turn down that sort of monopoly money without so much as a whimper certainly fits the bill. How many books are you going to have to sell to realise that sort of money?"

I shrugged. "What would I have done with it? Bought a bigger shop? A bigger shop means staff; staff means administration—national insurance and welfare headaches; assistants coming and going, being promoted or fired; partners, good ones and disasters . . . Is that what bookselling is all about? I came here because I *wanted* to . . . I don't want to *leave* . . ."

He smiled. "I'm proud of you, lad."

I felt curiously smug, as though teacher had patted me on the head. I didn't admit it was nothing to do with

100

my decision to reject the offer; nothing as reasoned as that. Goodman had simply annoyed me. Now that he was gone, I felt a prick of uneasiness. Who *was* Goodman, if that was his name? Had he really acted on an impulsive whim—or did he represent someone who wanted me out of the way—as the thugs in the stolen Jaguar had indicated in a different way?

On Tuesday I was surprised to receive a note from Caroline, enclosing photostats of receipts for the two books I had queried . . . surprised because the incident had completely slipped my mind. I had accepted her story and her reference to my suspicion of everyone and everything and the evidence now on my desk was a nagging reminder of the strained relationship we seemed to have now compared with what might have been. Dutifully I glanced at the photostats and compared them with my list of stolen books.

The Berridge copy of the Bunyan had been purchased by Henry's great-great-grandfather, George Berridge, in 1864 from the now defunct firm of Arthur Watkinson, Booksellers Row, London, on whose letterhead the receipt was issued, and had remained in the library ever since. The copy stolen from one of the Cambridge colleges had been purchased in 1848 by a Sir George West and bequeathed to the college on his death 28 years later. The receipt for the topographical book had been issued by the auctioneers James Lawrence & Son, Hanover Square, London following a sale conducted by them in 1873 while the stolen copy had been purchased by a Richard Simon at Bath in 1832 and donated to the Hudson Institute of Geographical Sciences in 1842.

Provided the receipts were genuine—and they looked authentic enough to me—I had obviously overreacted in the library. But before taking too much for granted I decided to lean on the experience of Frensham and phoned an account of what had happened. "Is there any way we could get a look under those bookplates if necessary?" I enquired.

He was pessimistic. "Only if we can lay our hands on them. Short of stealing them . . ." He broke off and after a lengthy silence continued ". . . that was intended as a joke! Do not, repeat not, take me literally. And there isn't a way of commandeering them—unless you have very strong grounds for supposing we'd find something . . ?"

"I haven't," I hastened to assure him.

"Then forget it, Matt. I'm very impressed with what you've done already. It's like throwing a stone into a pool and watching the ripples. The word must be getting around, particularly if you've quite accidentally made contact with someone who is actually involved. That person or persons is going to get rattled and when that happens they'll get careless. That incident with the river was the first mistake and when people start taking dangerous risks they leave themselves wide open."

I told him about the strange offer to buy the shop and my suspicion and he whistled under his breath. "I'm sure you're right. It's a small price to pay to protect their interests. Don't think in terms of £100,000 because when the heat was off they could sell it again and recoup quite a bit of that money."

As he talked it dawned on me for the first time that there could be a particular significance in these actions. If someone was anxious to stop the investigation why should he assume I would drop out simply because I left the area? As the robberies had been nationwide the implication must be that I was too close . . . *geographically* . . . to the heart of the matter. And yet, confusingly, the only two leads we had in the area were Heyman and Caroline. The thin man was obviously more deeply involved than he had admitted.

I was suddenly aware that Frensham was repeating a question. ". . . I said, would you object if I invited

Laura Cottingham to the theatre later this week? I have a spare ticket and can't think of a more delightful companion. But I wouldn't want to step out of line."

Laura Cottingham. She seemed light years away. My conscience wriggled uncomfrotably. Laura had been more than just a girl-friend; an extra word at the right moment and she might well have been sharing a home with me. Since setting eyes on Caroline Berridge I hadn't given Laura a thought, yet human nature being what it is I was instinctively possessive enough to hedge my bets. "Just theatre?" I queried.

"Dinner too, of course. Nothing else."

"That's fine with me," I announced complacently, making a mental note to ring her at the office after lunch. "I think I can trust you, Wilfred."

There was an embarrassed cough at the other end before he rang off. I did in fact telephone her later although I needed the incentive of knowing that there were enquiries I would need to make in London and that by travelling up on Friday it would be convenient to stay overnight at her flat. I can't remember when I was last as ashamed at making use of someone, let alone the girl for whom I had only recently felt so much warmth and affection.

Meanwhile Inspector Murdoch was something of an embarrassment because I had not yet reported Heyman's confession. I was worried that the police would stick to the rule-book and bring him in for questioning and doubted whether that would elicit any further information. Keeping the situation fluid, allowing him or others to react to my pressure, might be more productive. Yet I knew that if I didn't play 'ball' Murdoch could lean on me at any time and I preferred his co-operation to his enmity or even indifference. Besides I wondered whether the police had any luck yet in tracing the thugs in the stolen Jaguar.

Finally I took the bull by the horns and telephoned

him, apologising for the delay and reminding him that I was trying to conduct a business at the same time as the investigation. Fortunately Murdoch was apparently busy on a number of enquiries so his response was not as keen as I had feared. I gave him a full account of Heyman's confession, except the reference to Caroline Berridge, which I thought would only confuse the issue. I also decided not to mention the false alarm of the suspect books in the Oldham Park library nor the strange offer to buy my shop; I had a feeling about that but nothing else.

Murdoch seemed satisfied with my edited account. It was probably because he was so busy that he did not resist my suggestion of leaving Heyman to his own devices for the time being; keeping him under limited surveillance instead. Unfortunately he had little to report on the men in whom I was interested; having sent my description to Scotland Yard, he was now in their hands. I gathered from his tone that collaboration between the forces on anything other than major crimes left much to be desired.

During the week I'm generally in bed and asleep by midnight. Occasionally, however, preoccupied with a business or personal issue I've lain awake for hours. Still sensitive to the unfamiliar silence of a village at night and especially the eerie countryside stretching beyond my bedroom window, I found unexpected noise disproportionately disturbing and it would keep my senses on edge. In the early days the sound of a milk bottle disturbed by a prowling cat was enough to have me out of bed straight to the front of the building to peer out of the window. After several months I was not quite so easily alarmed but the sixth sense was still finely tuned. Three days after the visit from the mysterious Goodman I was dozing restlessly when what sounded like the creaking of a door hinge outside the bedroom window woke me with the jarring efficiency of an alarm-clock at my ear.

I looked at my wristwatch on the bedside cabinet, saw that it was one o'clock and lay back, listening intently. Apart from the pounding of my heart there was nothing to hear but I could not relax. I was not normally of a nervous disposition but the events of the past couple of weeks seemed to have sandpapered my instincts. Local youngsters, perhaps, breaking into my storeroom? I visualised the local variety of disenchanted youth and dismissed the thought; they wouldn't have the imagination. Telling myself that I was behaving like an old woman, I decided to take a look. Quietly I put on my shoes and trousers—without which no Englishman would ever contemplate dealing with intruders—and crept downstairs. I did not bother to arm myself, partly because I had convinced myself I was making a fuss over nothing and partly because I was capable of tackling the sort of burglar one might find in these neck of the woods. I had been taught to deal with *trained* men, terrorists and their like, opponents I would regard as equals in a fight.

Relying on the element of surprise, I crept downstairs, carefully avoiding the steps I knew creaked. In the private room below I used as a study and to keep my reference books there was a window overlooking the garden but I would see nothing outside. Apart from the shop in the front with its wide frontage, there was another bookroom accessible to customers, with a glass door leading to the store area beyond, also filled with books. That door was locked at night although the place was of course vulnerable to anyone intending to break-in. Not moving, I listened intently from sounds coming from the storeroom. It was so quiet that I was on the point of concluding I had imagined or misinterpreted the original sound when I heard a muted squeal, instantly recognisable as a glass cutter. I crept nearer and carefully opened the door to the bookroom a few inches. I couldn't see anything because the glass door was hidden at right angles but I caught the diffused beam of a torch and I could now hear but not decipher whispers, indicating that there were at least two people outside.

Deciding to play safe, I retreated quietly into the shop to find something which might be used as a weapon. There were in fact the decorative antique guns and swords on the walls but I hesitated over using them. My reverence for antiquity made me think twice about the prospect of breaking the butt of one of those beautiful guns over the head of some moronic thug, while the heavy crossed swords simply looked *too* dangerous. I did not wish to find myself facing a manslaughter charge. Instead I favoured a two foot long poker from the fireplace and went back to ambush the intruders.

They were inside the house now and talking in whispers but I was suddenly more aware of the distinctive smell of paraffin. Now, for the first time, I was alarmed. I could feel the adrenalin flowing as I stood, transfixed, trying to decide my next move. There was no point in continuing the cat and mouse game if they intended to make use of that paraffin. I listened anxiously for further sounds but they had stopped talking. Then there were the noises of paper being torn and crumpled and the more ominous one of liquid gurgling as the metal container in which it was housed was systematically emptied. It was obvious they were going to set fire to the building.

The barbarity of mindlessly destroying antiquarian books, irrespective of monetary value—quite apart from the possible murder of me, supposedly asleep above—momentarily clouded my judgement. I was on the point of bursting in and possibly killing the arsonists responsible when I was stopped in my tracks by the

106

sudden appearance of one of them, carrying a two gallon can in his right hand, presumably intending to prepare another room for destruction. Despite my preparedness I was so consumed with fury that I reacted sluggishly although fortunately the intruder was even more startled at finding me. At the time we both seemed to respond in slow motion but it could only have been a split second.

I remember that he opened his mouth to yell a warning and I took action to silence him. My instincts in control, I went for his right side, where he was encumbered by the weight of the bulky container, too heavy to use as a weapon. Sensing my intention, he dropped the can but too late to stop the backhanded smash of the poker against the side of his head. The warning shout turned into a strangled cry of pain and I caught him with a forehanded follow-up before he hit the ground.

The occupants of the bookroom were still 'frozen' in the reaction to their companion's cry when I leapt among them. One was the thick-set man I remembered instantly as an occupant of the Jaguar which had forced me off the road. In close-up for the first time I saw that he had what appeared to be a razor scar down one side of his face. In fact he looked what he was, a hard man, but at that moment inconsequentially I thought of him only in context of the car chase and wondered whether he was accompanied now by the long-haired youth who had impressed me with his driving skills. I didn't recognise the young man with him now but I would in the future. He was petrified by my sudden explosive arrival and, I imagined, the poker in my hand. But if I needed any incentive it was provided by the memory of my experience in the river and I made straight for Scarface, determined to settle an old score first. He showed no fear or emotion of any sort and stepped forward to meet me, yelling to his companion. "I'll deal with him—you just get the fire going. And quick about it!"

Both men were dressed entirely black—matching trousers, polo-necked jumpers and gloves—indicating they had come prepared. But they had little else in common. Scarface was obviously a hardened professional, his companion no more than a willing apprentice, a scrawny young man not accustomed to thinking for himself. With only a momentary frightened glance at me he pulled a cigarette lighter from a trousers' pocket, flicked the top and held the resultant flame to a pile of papers on the floor. Desperately I switched targets and as he stooped to light the papers I kicked him in the chest, actually aiming for his throat but missing. Even so, the force knocked him off balance and he dropped the lighter, the flame going out. I kicked it away and almost in the same movement stamped my heel hard on the hand that had just relinquished it. He screamed with pain and I repeated the dose, conscious of the delicate bones at the back of his hand snapping under the pressure. He was otherwise unhurt but I doubted whether he would have much stomach for any subsequent fight. He clutched desperately his wrist and whimpered with pain, so that his older companion shouted at him to shut up and get out. "See if George is all right and then both get out." He had a marked Cockney accent, a further indication that he was not a local man.

I let the youngster go and turned to face Scarface, who had slipped a pair of knuckle dusters over his fists. He moved towards me in a cautious but relaxed stance, seeming to be in his element, the traditional 'heavy', the enforcer, the hard man. I could detect from his expression that he regarded me simply as a nuisance to be despatched quickly, so that he could complete what he had come to do, alone; the loss of his companions obviously not worrying him in the slightest. Even as I weighed him up a jolting straight left jab, weighted with the 'dusters', caught me high on the right shoulder with numbing force and I knew another like that would incapacitate my right arm, nullifying the value of the poker. For a moment I cursed my inhibitions over bringing a sword. The untended edges had blunted over the years but I was angry enough now to decapitate him with a couple of strokes.

Instead I used the poker as a long dagger, slipping inside the next punch and ramming the 'point' into his midriff. It was not sharp in the same way as a dagger but the impact of an iron rod, concentrated in a diameter of less than ¼ inch, was enough to pierce the flesh. The force halted him in mid-stride and the shock and sickness that must have followed instantly caused him to stagger. I grabbed one of his limp arms, twisted and hauled him off-balance and pulled him over my shoulder. The weight of his sprawling mass colliding with a bookshelf, pulled it away from the wall and the books stacked there cascaded down. Irrationally, the sight of further damage fuelled my rage. From his position on the floor he tried to focus on me but was too dazed. Yet I was angry enough to leap on top of him and begin banging his head on the floor. I might have killed him, I suppose, if someone had not hit me over the head with a chair.

The room began to swim and I thought incongruously of those Hollywood Westerns in which chairs used in saloon bar fights always disintegrate like matchsticks. This one seemed as solid as a rock and the impact probably never even cracked its coat of varnish but I felt a terrible pain inside my head, an overwhelming tiredness and indifference to everything. I collapsed on to my knees and fought desperately to stay awake. Luckily the youth was too scared to stay and finish me off, concerned only with shepherding his more seriously hurt companions to safety. I wanted to stop them but although I was apparently conscious I found I could not even open my eyes, let alone get to my feet. Incredibly, apart from the desire to stay awake, nothing else seemed to matter.

It was not until much later that I wondered how they got away. They would have brought a car but the youth had an incapacitated hand which would make driving difficult and one of his companions was suffering from possible concussion and the other with head and probable internal injuries. They would have good cause to remember me.

SEVEN

For the first time since I'd stopped smoking ten years before, I found I was actually biting my nails. Over-excitement, of course. I was so 'high' I might have been stuffed to the eyeballs with benzedrine. Yet that mind-blowing feeling of exhilaration was curiously unsatisfying since it was also impossible to relax; not even enough to go back to bed, let alone sleep. The scene was played back in my mind, with total recall even to the most irrelevant minutia, so that the unending repetition became a nightmare verging on physical distress.

If I could have spoken to someone, to have let it all out, it might have been different. But it would have been pointless—not to say bloody selfish—to have got Frensham or Murdoch out of bed. What could they have said or done? I did seriously consider dialling 999, to alert the police for rats scampering back to London, since I was convinced that was where they came from. But even then I hesitated—for no good reason other than a strange feeling of possessiveness; that it was *my* battle and that I could win it alone, without their ham-fisted interference.

I had a bad headache too but it was not until I had taken a warm shower and dried myself that I discovered blood on the towel from a cut at the back of my scalp. The blood had congealed and luckily the wound did not start to bleed again. But, reassured on that score, I became increasingly aware of a spreading bruise at my right shoulder. Yet, incredibly, in the excitement of my first fight in several years I'd suffered no discomfort at all until taking the shower.

I got dressed and made myself a pot of tea and a

111

couple of slices of toast. It was nearly 4 am. I thought about the arsonists. The most significant factor was that the leader—I had begun to think of him as Scarface—had been in the car which manoeuvred me into the river. The incidents therefore had to be connected, along with the offer to buy the shop. Someone wanted me out of the way because of what I had discovered—or was threatening to find out. I concentrated on him. Scarface was no book thief, at least not by inclination. Thief probably; villain certainly; if anything almost a caricature of the armed robbery specialist. But that was not the sort of man one imagined carrying out a series of break-ins at bookshops and libraries unless there was something else involved. Who was he? On the face of it not 'Mr Big' although probadly a key figure in some criminal organisation. Where? The south-west was hardly a hotbed of vice and gangsterdom and the only gangs of significant size were probably in London. Indeed, 'gangland', if such a place existed, was unfamiliar territory but I had a feeling there had to be a link with someone who knew me or knew of my investigation. The only person who might have such connections was Billy Lloyd, who, as a top professional boxer, had seen the sort of celebrity to attract under- world admirers. As a successful businessman, with a fortune earned through legitimate means, I could not see *why* he would still saddle himself with crooks—but that was really beside the point.

Inspector Murdoch was the obvious person with whom to compare notes but I was reluctant to confide in him. I had no illusions about the craggy inspector; he had indulged me so far because it suited his purpose. He would have no compunction in brushing me aside when he was ready to take action off his own bat. I thought instead of my former colleagues on the Daily Chronicle, with whom I could probably work some sort of deal. In my investigation of the Seeley murder case I had spent some time with George Kester, the paper's talented gossip columnist, and through him I might now pick the brains of the sports and crime specialists. I waited impatiently until it was light and phoned Kester at home. My job on the paper had been personal assistant to the chairman, another name for 'trouble shooter', and perhaps because I wasn't a journalist I had never really got close to Kester. But we had co-existed through an unpleasant period, established some common ground and emerged with a degree of mutual respect.

I told him my assignment and offered an exclusive story for the Chronicle in exchange for his co-operation, and his journalistic curiosity got the better of him. He was even more aware than me that the story might never materialise but it was a calculated gamble and he had nothing to lose but his time. What I needed was comprehensive information on Billy Lloyd and his business career since retiring from the ring. I also asked him for anything the paper had on Oldham Park and Lord and Lady Berridge. After promising to be at his office by mid-morning I telephoned Laura Cottingham to see if she would be free later in the day.

"Matt who . . ?" she enquired cynically.

"The prospective client," I suggested, "the one you should be nice to . . ." I assumed a Welsh accent. "Matt the Book . . ."

"Book the Matt? . . . Book mat? I used to know a *door* mat . . !"

I mentally groaned. It was going to be tough. "That's the one," I conceded. "Apart from anything else, you were interested in my advertising account."

"I remember now," she said with pointed vagueness. "But that was *years* ago. We don't need any more clients at the moment, thank you."

"Would you turn away big money?" I protested. "I'm even prepared to go to dinner and wine . . ."

She sighed. "You country boys certainly know how to sweep a girl off her feet. How could I resist such sophistication, such charm, such breathtaking *generosity* . . ?"

"Very funny," I interrupted. "You've made your point. I'll pick you up at seven . . ."

"Fine," she declared. "Will that be October 17 or November 20?" She paused to reflect and added, "I see that December 3 is free too, if you care to book now."

It wasn't just an act. She was genuinely annoyed, and with some justification, so I prepared to eat humble pie. I apologised for my recent silence, giving her a potted account of all the things that had happened. "If you would have dinner with me tonight I'd attempt to explain that what you assumed was strange behaviour was really only a total commitment to the investigation." When she did not respond I added, "You have every right to be annoyed and if necessary I will wait until October. But surely there's no need for you to sink to my level . . ."

"Oh, I accept your apology," she said. "You're forgiven—but don't expect me to change my plans for tonight just because you happen to be in London and at a loose end. I only do that for special people."

I winced. She *was* angry. Either I had to accept it gracefully or fight back, no holds barred. Despite my current preoccupation, not to say infatuation, with Caroline Berridge I was too fond of Laura to allow the rift to widen. Throwing integrity to the winds, I used repentance as a feint and proceeded to hit below the belt.

"Fair enough," I appeared to concede. "Let's forget it—it's ridiculously short notice. I didn't know until five minutes ago I'd be in town. The local hospital want a second opinion and there's no point in waiting."

Laura did not reply until I was on the point of throwing in the towel and when she did the cynicism

114

had been replaced by uncertainty. "What were you doing at the hospital?"

My brain raced to embellish the lie. "Nothing to worry about," I said confidently. "I was attacked last night. Some people broke in . . . something to do with the investigation; we're getting too close for someone's comfort . . ."

"You're obviously in one piece?" she said cautiously.

"Obviously," I admitted. "You should know better than to ask. Anyone who has the temerity to attack me is lucky to survive with his life."

"I realise that. They must have been mad, reckless fools. But presumably someone got lucky before he expired . . ?" There was an element of concern in her voice.

"It's just another X-ray." Even as I said it the lie seemed so transparent. Why, for example, could not 'another X-ray' be done locally? But Laura trusted me of course. The anxiety was apparent in her voice when she replied almost aggressively, like a parent concealing worry over an accident-prone child. "What will you do after the hospital?"

I managed to inject a pathetic shrug into my answer. "Drive back to Ardley, I expect . . ."

"That's ridiculous," she interrupted. "You probably shouldn't be driving at all. What's wrong with the train?"

"You know me, I can't bear to sit around doing nothing."

"Then at least you should stay the night."

"If you're offering to put me up, thanks very much. It *would* be less of a strain."

She hesitated. "I wasn't but it seems foolish wasting money on a hotel." She stopped for a moment and then added guardedly, "You *have* been telling me the truth?"

I felt sick at the deception and salved my conscience

with a compromise answer, the truthful part of my story: "They tried to set fire to the shop. Three of them. Luckily I woke up and caught them in time."

"God, that *was* lucky. Knowing how you feel about the shop, it was probably worth a broken arm or two . . ."

"Or three," I confirmed. "I'll tell you about it later. Any chance of breaking your date?"

"I don't have one. You'd better come over just after seven and I'll prepare a meal here."

"That's wonderful, but we'll go out. It's the least I can do."

George Kester was a thickset, prematurely bald man who conformed to the layman's image of a newspaper columnist and, it's been said, tried to act the part. He had run the Daily Chronicle's gossip column for the past fifteen years, since his early twenties—very young by Fleet Street standards in those days. It was generally considered that his impressive talent was out of proportion to the content of popular papers like the Chronicle but for some indefinable reason the paper managed to instill a strong loyalty among its editorial staff. He was never without a cigarette although he generally smoked about half and filled the ashtray with a mountain of giant stubs. The picture reminded me a little of Heyman but whereas the librarian chain-smoked through nerves Kester's vices seemed to be endured principally to maintain his image of the tough, dissolute journalist. His mouth constantly grimaced, for example, with the taste of whisky, which he appeared to use more as a mouthwash than a drink, because his consumption of alcohol was quite high and he was never drunk.

He greeted me with a coffee but then sent me straight up to the cuttings and picture library so that I could go through the paper's printed record of Billy Lloyd and

Oldham Park, and I had good reason to be grateful for his common sense. The cuttings—news and feature reports and interviews—are kept by all newspapers to assist their reporters with background for each new assignment and through them I was able to build up a fairly comprehensive picture of Lloyd's path from novice amateur boxer to the celebrity he now was. Not surprisingly, there was nothing in the files about Caroline Berridge and not much more about her husband, apart from a short piece when he inherited the title. Oldham Park merely merited a few pop festival pictures.

Lloyd's story was fascinating, even though most of the detail came from personal interviews and we only had his word that the facts were correct. It appears that he was born and bred in the East End of London. He was only twelve when his mother died but old enough to mourn her passing; apparently he did not have the same regard for his father, who remained a shadowy figure through the interviews. Bright at school, he was befriended and taken in hand by a sports master who recognised some indefinable talent, strong enough to lift him out of the gutter—given an opportunity. However this was not manifest in his academic work and it was his success as an amateur boxer that encouraged him to turn professional. The schoolmaster and a boxing writer friend were given credit for finding a shrewd and honest young manager who would not exploit him. And from him Billy learnt more than boxing; the value of saving and more particularly the benefit of shrewd investment, making use of the money that was beginning to roll in. Having reached contender status, but, because of his looks, personality and dynamic style, with a following greater than the champion, Billy was surprisingly KO'd.

In common with past champions he had come back brilliantly after that defeat, overwhelming several class fighters before finally being stopped by a top American. To use his own words, Lloyd suddenly realised the folly of getting knocked about when he was capable of identifying ways of making as much money by using his brain. Coming up in the world, he unashamedly admitted taking elocution lessons to broaden his circle. Learning quickly and gradually outstripping his mentors, Billy had gone from success to success. Starting with boutiques, areas where his personality could be used to advantage, he moved into property and share-dealings. These days he was known and respected more in the City than by the public at large, who remembered only the young hopeful who had dashed their dreams of bringing a world title to Britain.

When I returned to the little goldfish bowl that distinguished Kester, the columnist, from the reporters he introduced me first to Don White, the paper's sports writer, a small, dark, intense man, surprisingly chubby for one who obviously burnt energy at a tremendous pace. We'd never met but when we were introduced he remembered my name and the circumstances in which I had left the paper. Kester merely said I was 'interested' in Bill Lloyd and since White did not seem terribly curious I didn't bother to elaborate. The boxer obviously revived pleasant memories for him. "He was a natural . . . an irresistible force," he began, as though that summed up all I needed to know.

"Then why didn't he win even a British title?" I asked.

He shrugged. "Who knows? He chucked it in pretty early; he *might* have gone on to become the British champion. But you can speculate for ever on what might have been."

Kester interjected. "I used to follow his progress. I agree—he seemed to have it all, except perhaps a knock-out punch, at least at world-class level."

"That's true. He'd wear them down. But that's true

of several men who went on to become world champions. Rocky Marciano never lost a fight and he had much the same style."

"Why then?" I persisted.

"My own theory," said White, "is that he was too intelligent for his own good. A professional boxer has to be absolutely fearless and Billy was as brave as they come—I've seen him cut to pieces and go on to win—but he was suspect against the KO specialist. I reckon that at the back of his mind, deep down in his subconscious, was the knowledge which would only worry an intelligent guy—that just *one* punch can scramble your brains permanently."

"A subconscious fear of getting hurt?" suggested Kester.

"Not so much a fear, as an awareness. I can remember a world class fighter you've probably never heard of, who got to the top through extraordinary boxing skills—the sort of talent we see only once in a lifetime."

"Like Ali," I speculated.

"An even better boxer but he was only a welterweight and too quiet a chap ever to make much money. But he was a true boxing master . . . sort of bloke who would defy you to hit him with his feet tied together—and you couldn't, of course. But he had a fatal flaw in his make-up—what they call in the boxing fraternity a glass jaw. When they did land a lucky punch on his chin, he'd be knocked out. His record showed that those defeats were only at the hands of punchers of some repute. Much later he admitted it was psychological. The *knowledge* that a single blow was capable of killing him was enough for his subconscious to metaphorically throw in the towel."

"You mean give up?"

"No, he'd actually lose consciousness. You know the power of the mind. It can literally kill or cure."

Kester laughed. "So there is an element of truth in those old cartoons of the wide-boy manager shoving smelling salts under the nose of his punch-drunk fighter; saying 'he can't hurt *us*'. If someone can be kidded he'll fight on when he's got no chance?"

"Exactly. He'll even protest if the referee intervenes. The highly intelligent man doesn't need the referee to tell him he's in danger. I'm not talking about cuts and bruises but about serious injury, brain damage and the like."

Kester pulled a face. "Probably shouldn't have been a fighter in the first place. If he'd been born with that old silver spoon, who knows what he might have accomplished? If he'd gone into politics he might have been on the way to becoming Prime Minister."

"He's not doing too badly without those advantages," interjected White. "Some people thrive on having it tough." He glanced at his watch pointedly and as though on cue Arthur Holman, the crime reporter, stuck his head round the door. "You wanted me, gentlemen?" White looked up, smiled happily and excused himself and Holman took his place. Holman and I knew each other slightly but he was a little more suspicious of my interest in Billy Lloyd than the sports writer had been.

"I don't know what you're after," he declared, "but Lloyd is quite clean. I've never even heard a whisper . . . and I'm not short of contacts."

"It's not him so much as his associates," I pointed out. "He's a respectable businessman these days, admittedly, but I'm trying to find out whether he still has any links with . . . let's say disreputable characters; people he wouldn't take to the Lord Mayor's banquet?"

"Not as far as I know," said Holman. "Or that he ever did. Of course all sports and showbiz celebrities have their share of underworld hangers-on. He probably had *more* than his share when he was in that

120

world but I'm sure he left all that behind, probably on the day he moved out of the family council flat. Why do you want to know?"

I shrugged. "It's just a hunch. I had a brush with a couple of thugs. For certain reasons I can't go into at the moment I think they may have been friends of Billy Lloyd. I've promised George that the Chronicle will be the first to know if I can ever prove it."

"Do you have any names?"

"No." I laughed sheepishly. "I gave a description to the local police and they're supposed to have checked with the Met but no dice so far. Perhaps it wasn't detailed enough."

He volunteered to have a go and I told him about the long-haired youth, driver of the Jaguar, and Scarface, with whom I'd had a second meeting. He shook his head blankly after the first account but when I listed the distinguishing features of Scarface his eyes narrowed and I could see that it rang a bell. Without saying anything he picked up George's phone and dialled an internal number. "Arthur here. Do you remember the time the agency bloke had that run-in with a bodyguard and had his camera smashed? Andy got a beautiful picture of the incident. Can I see it? No . . . I'm with George Kester. Get a boy to bring it round."

He put the phone down and explained what had been obvious—that he had spoken to Picture Desk. "Your description struck a chord. There was a time when Lloyd was going around with that Hollywood actress, Monica Winters . . . quite a few Hollywood actresses, come to think of it. But she was fussy about what got back to her husband in the States. As you've just heard, one of the agencies took a picture and up popped this bodyguard to teach him a lesson. Smashed the camera and took the film. Could be the bloke you described."

"Great. Who was he bodyguard to . . ? The woman or Lloyd?"

"Lloyd, presumably. It was his territory, so to speak."

I crossed my fingers and Kester noticed the gesture. "That doesn't mean much. Probably needs a bodyguard. Every yobbo with a few beers under his belt reckons he can beat the pro fighter . . ."

"I agree," interjected Holman. "Makes life a bit more difficult for us but I can't see the difference between the police or special branch officer attached to politicians or the private guard paid by someone who can afford it."

I shrugged. "I'm not arguing. But it depends on the bodyguard."

A boy knocked timidly at Kester's door and brought in the photograph. Holman studied it for a moment, nodded to confirm that this was what he had remembered and then passed it to me. The black-and-white still showed a photographer losing his camera to a bulky man in dark evening suit, complete with black bow tie. The clothes were unfamiliar but the face was instantly recognisable. It was Scarface.

"That's the same man," I confirmed. "Do we know his name?"

Holman looked pleased with himself. "Bobby Miles. Used to work for the Collett gang before they all went down for about twenty years apiece."

"How did he get off then?" I asked.

Holman smiled. "Christ knows. Could have been luck; could have been a smart lawyer. There was some talk of a deal with the police. That's probably what happened. If the Law had been upset they would have gone for him at every opportunity but as far as I know they've left him alone."

"What's his connection with Billy Lloyd?"

He shrugged. "You'll have to ask him yourself . . . Lloyd, that is. I wouldn't want to ask Miles anything."

Rather to my surprise Billy Lloyd agreed to see me

that afternoon. My excuse about just happening to be in town seemed incredibly lame but his manner was charming. He behaved in fact as though he had nothing planned for the afternoon—which I realised was unlikely to be the case—and could think of nothing more enjoyable than a social chat with me. He lived in a huge white Edwardian house just off Regents Park. It looked more like a foreign legation than the home of a single man and when I expressed my interest at the size he volunteered to show me round.

The basement had been converted into a gymnasium, with an adjoining shooting gallery, which I noticed was adequately soundproofed. In the ground-floor living area there was a separate games room in which he had installed a full-size snooker table. Both areas had the appearance of being regularly used, confirming my impression that Loyd was not the sort of person who did things for show.

The rest of the ground floor was used for his business purposes, with a large, landscaped reception area housing three attractive secretaries, all working industriously and again obviously not for show. Recessed at one end was an impressive array of filing cabinets. An imposing inner office complete with teleprinter, large photocopier and battery of telephones was the domain of Lloyd's private secretary, a woman he introduced as Mrs Summers. In contrast, his own office was quite small. French windows and a balcony overlooked the park and the room was equipped more as a lounge than executive suite although a large coffee-table, surrounded by easy-chairs in sumptuous leather, obviously served as a discussion area. The upper floor housed the main living-room and what he dismissed airily as guest bedrooms.

When we returned to his office Mrs Summers, one of those quietly efficient 'anonymous' secretaries, produced a tray with tea in silver pot and exquisite china tableware. I wondered if he had chosen them or whether he left such decisions to a designer. The whole place had a professional touch about it but Lloyd matched it perfectly. On reflection, my use of 'but' is revealing; I have to admit there was a tinge of envy in my appraisal. It was nothing to do with his success. I'd never been interested in making money so his affluence and authority did not disturb me. It was more to do with his influence over Caroline Berridge. Why couldn't he have been an elderly friend of the family instead of being so physically attractive as well as so damn' likeable? Even the slight air of smugness that had irritated me initially at Oldham Park had disappeared. Here, at the control centre of his own empire, he was completely relaxed and natural. I was dressed informally as usual but in comparison with his shirtsleeved neatness I felt almost scruffy, as though I should have freshened up after my pub lunch with Kester and his cronies. Then I reminded myself that I was making enquiries into a series of robberies in which he might be implicated and began to look at him in a more dispassionate light.

We fenced with generalities during the tea, after which he told his secretary we were not to be disturbed for—he checked his watch, looked briefly at me and added "twenty minutes" unless something important arose. When she had closed the door I told him how impressed I was with the set-up. "I didn't realise quite how close you were to your business."

"There's only one way to make money and that's to be single-minded," he said in a matter-of-fact tone.

"But presumably you're not completely tied—I've seen you at Oldham Park, for example."

"That was partly business too but if you mean 'how tied am I?' the answer is not simple. I've earned the right to be my own master. *I* come first, not the business, but since we're inseparable in most situations

124

our interests inevitably coincide. I put in the hours necessary but they don't have to be conventional office hours. I might be in here at midnight or all day Sunday. I'm never really out of touch, even away from London. There's a phone in the car so I can be reached even between appointments. Anyway, you wanted to see me, so fire away. We've just wasted a couple of your minutes, I'm afraid."

I had thought about the discussion in the car, driving to London, and had got most satisfaction in those mock interviews by putting my cards on the table, telling him I suspected his involvement and asking him to deny it. But when it came to the real-life situation I lost my nerve. The allegation seemed too far-fetched, and libellous if he wanted to be nasty. Instead I asked about his relationship with the Berridges.

"Do they know you're asking these questions?" he enquired quite mildly.

"No," I admitted, "but I wouldn't try to conceal it, I'm dealing with a number of robberies and it so happens that a couple were literally on my doorstep— one of them, as you know, at Oldham Park. I've no leads whatsoever so I have to start by relating places like Oldham Park and its library to the outside, particularly the book world . . . how well-known the collection might have been . . . the sort of people who would have known about it and might have been tempted. Some of this I've already established from Caroline Berridge but in general business areas I thought I might get a more realistic picture from an independent business authority, such as yourself. It's difficult to ask Lord Berridge, for example, if he's capable of keeping his head above water."

Lloyd smiled. "I don't see why not. At least he wouldn't guess why you'd really asked the question . . ."

"And why would that have been?"

"To find out if he was desperate enough to sell or steal his own books?"

I nodded. ". . . A theory I've already dismissed as being out of character."

"Exactly. Henry has rather different values to most of us. He might shoot a man as a matter of honour but he'd never entertain the slightest whisper of dishonesty.

"And that applies to Caroline too, I imagine?"

He laughed. "Except that Caroline wouldn't hurt a fly either."

I looked at my watch. "I'm not getting very good value for my twenty minutes. What about their financial situation?"

He shrugged. "They'll survive. As she told you, Oldham Park is a millstone, but with her creative energy behind it it'll stay afloat."

"She tended to give *you* most of the credit."

"I'm just the backstop. Did you know how I came to meet the Berridges?" I shook my head and he explained: "I met Caroline at a reception organised by the advertising agency we share. She stood out in a place bulging with dolly birds—and 'bulging' is the appropriate word. So naturally I made a beeline for her . . . not that, as I quickly discovered, she was a pushover like the others . . ."

I said nothing and he studied me for a second before breaking into a grin. "Go on, you poker-faced bugger. You're dying to ask—what's the relationship now?"

I felt a constriction in my throat, embarrassed that my thoughts were so easy to read. I forced a stiff smile. "The thought had crossed my mind," I conceded.

"Come off it," he persisted. "You fancy her like mad. It's written all over you."

I was tempted for a hysterical moment to share his intimacy, to be lads together and make a conventional joke about her sexual attributes, but I pulled myself together. I was too ashamed of my vulnerability to be

126

anything but evasive. "You just said I was poker-faced. I find her attractive, admittedly, but that's as far as it goes."

His mocking smile disappeared. "Just as well. The lady isn't available. I tried of course but she made it clear it was Henry Berridge alone . . . till death do them part. And I wasn't prepared to go that far."

I was reserving judgement on that statement but couldn't resist replying, "So you're just good friends?"

"Something like that," he said mockingly. "But don't let it worry you. I don't like to boast but with all due respect to Lady Berridge, who is a dear friend, I wasn't exactly short of consolation. Besides, when I got to meet Henry I found we had quite a bit in common. We're from different worlds, perhaps, but we've arrived at the same place. We're both mad on guns although I prefer target shooting. I don't believe in killing anything unnecessarily and of course he thinks I'm bloody queer. Occasionally I'll go for a rabbit shoot with him and his mates—because I know we're doing the farmer a favour—but generally I stick to clay-pigeons or even hand-guns."

"I raise my hat to you," I acknowledged. "I'm slightly squeamish about blood sports myself."

He shrugged. "I've no objection to blood or even killing. The operative word is 'unnecessarily'." Our eyes met and I wondered for a moment whether he had intended the remark as a threat. But what did he have to threaten me about?

I realised I was not going to get anything from Lloyd—if indeed there was anything to uncover. The more I thought about his business empire and giant turnover involved, the more difficult it was to reconcile his possible involvement in robberies which were in comparison 'peanuts'. He knew nothing about books so why should he involve himself with others—men from such different worlds as Heyman's, for example—when

127

he could do his own thing?

The loose ends were his association with Bobby Miles. I asked him, phrasing the question as discreetly as I could, telling him why I was interested and recouting my two meetings with the man. "I understand he's a friend of yours?"

He frowned. "Who told you that?" When I didn't answer he raised his eyebrows. "Whoever it was, you've been misinformed."

"I've seen a photograph of you together . . . the impression was that he worked for you at some time . . ?"

He laughed and waved a hand to encompass the office and the building. "Where would he fit into this? He's a character from my boxing days. Did me one or two favours and I'm inclined to remember things like that . . . try to return them when I can."

"And you haven't seen him recently?"

He frowned. "Don't make a meal of it. I told you—we don't mix in the same circles."

I dug my heels in. "I accept that—please don't misunderstand me. It's Miles I'm interested in, not you. If I suggested that he was mixed up in the robberies in some way—pretty obvious, since he's attacked me twice—would you be surprised?"

"Nothing surprises me."

"Would you know where I could find him?"

He shook his head. "I wouldn't tell you if I knew. Besides, you're talking about a period of my life I prefer to forget. Does *that* surprise you?"

"Not at all. I'm not too happy with some of my past."

He grimaced. "The chances are that, whatever it is you regret, it was at least your *choice* in the first place. I had no choice. The only things I can remember with nostalgia, let alone affection, is my mother who died when I was still a kid and my young sister. The rest . . ." He shrugged and shook his head. "It's none of your business."

I was interested in anything that might show some light on his relationship with Miles so I persisted. "I must admit I did some research on you before I came. In the various interviews you've been very reticent about your childhood, particularly your father . . . Is he still alive?"

He stared at me for a moment, undecided whether to terminate the discussion or accept an opportunity to unburden himself. Eventually he gave a cynical laugh. "Why don't I talk about my old man? Because he doesn't merit the time it takes. I don't even hate the bastard. If he'd beaten me regularly I might have had something to focus on but he was a nothing. My mother died prematurely, worn out looking after him as well as us kids. And when she passed on, instead of coming to his senses, he used the excuse to drown his sorrows—in the pub. We had to bring ourselves up. My sister, Ethel—she was two years older than me—did her best and both of us looked after the little 'un, our Dorothy. Ethel, can't blame her, I suppose, turned out a hard nut, married the first bloke who came along and left us to the old man. Dorothy went to live with my aunt and soon as I started earning a bit of cash I took over that responsibility . . . saw her through art college. Turned out a real darling, thank God."

"But what was so terrible about him? Or was it just weakness?" I asked.

He shrugged. "Probably. I suppose I'm as irrational as the next guy when it comes to likes and dislikes. He probably meant well in his way but he didn't *do* a bloody thing, and what he even thought was for the best would have been disastrous if I'd listened. When I was eighteen he tried to marry me off to a local girl— daughter of one of his mates . . . pretty kid but thick as two planks. Only reason was that she'd inherited a corner grocery shop and he thought I was on to a good thing . . . security and all that. Me. Of course when I made the big time as a pro it went to his head. Changed from being a nothing—but at least an inoffensive nothing—into a big-headed ruffian always getting into fights. It got so bad that I had to threaten to lay one on him if he didn't stop. No, he was no friend of mine."

"I take your point. And Miles—he's part of that era . . ?"

Lloyd looked at his watch and stood up. "I've told you things I've never told a soul. I'd be obliged if you'd keep it to yourself."

I nodded. "Thanks for sparing the time."

His eyes held mine. "I like you. We could be friends but I doubt if we ever will." He smiled. "But I'm sure we'll bump into each other . . . around."

I doubted it but nodded agreeably. We shook hands and I left.

EIGHT

The moment we saw each other, the tension eased. We embraced, instinctively and with warmth. Then, taking a deep breath, I told Laura the true reason for my trip to London, admitting the story about a hospital check-up had been a ploy in what I considered desperate circumstances. But now the relationship was back to normal she merely laughed and conceded she was relieved that I cared enough.

We went to dinner at the Connaught, spending money I could scarcely afford as though it was a penance. But the meal was of course excellent and Laura's company as captivating as ever. She was the sort of woman with whom I had always felt totally relaxed and we had spent many hours listening to music or reading, not needing speech to communicate. When she was in a talkative mood she was quite enchanting, as Frensham and others before him had discovered. Yet as the evening drew to a close and I asked for the bill I began to feel apprehensive about the night ahead.

For all her frivolity and air of independence, I realised now that Laura loved me. I wondered if I was being fair to her. I studied her face as she chattered on, oblivious of my qualms. She was strikingly beautiful, warm-hearted, intelligent and the perfect companion—everything I had ever sought in a woman. But as I watched her I became increasingly uneasy. No question that I loved her but there was something missing. I thought suddenly of Caroline Berridge and my stomach turned over. That was it! I could never have studied her so dispassionately. I knew it was to her I wanted to make love tonight, not Laura. I dreaded the pretence, the subterfuge, yet I would have to stay the night and doubted if I could find an excuse that would not be hurtful.

I was cold and miserable by the time we had driven back but Laura's mood was too euphoric for her to notice. Her two-bedroom flat was on the fifth floor of a luxury block—the sort where the service fee includes a change of fresh flowers in the foyer every two or three days—at the back of Marble Arch. Laura had been earning good money for several years so the rent would not have presented any headaches but the value of the lease must have been staggering and I had an idea she had raised that money from the proceeds of a legacy. It was furnished with style, taste and a care that indicated she would not lightly leave.

She opened the front door and the first thing I noticed was an envelope on the mat. It was unstamped, which was hardly surprising since the last delivery had been mid-morning, and I picked it up. Astonishingly, it was addressed to me. Written in biro, the letters were printed untidily as though by an illiterate—or someone wanting to disguise his handwriting. I was immediately uneasy. Nobody knew I would be here and anyone who suspected I might have been would surely have telephoned. Frensham perhaps? He was the only person who knew about Laura and some of my likely movements but he would surely not have written as badly as that.

Only vaguely aware of the note and not having seen the writing, Laura had made straight for the kitchen. I heard the kettle being filled from the tap and then she called out, "Is that another mini-cab circular? They're always telling me how cheap it is to get to London Airport. I *never* go to London Airport."

I didn't answer. I tore open the envelope and pulled out a page of lined notepaper. Stuck on in some semblance of a pattern were cut-out pieces of newsprint of different types and sizes. But the message was clear.

> "Miss Cottingham is a pretty girl.
> If you want her to stay that way,
> forget about the books. That's in
> the past—think of the future and
> do the lady a favour."

I stood on the doormat, petrified. What had I done?
Suddenly Laura was framed in the kitchen doorway,
surprised at my preoccupation. "You look pretty sick.
Was it from a rapturous admirer? I should have warned
you, I get them all the time." She held out a hand for the
note.

I put it back in my breast pocket and smiled briefly.
"It was addressed to me, actually. Personal . . ."

"Matt . . ? I don't believe you," she said, wrinkling
her brow. "Unless you told anyone you were coming
here?"

I contemplated trying to bluff but my conscience
rebelled. I had lied enough to her and now through me
she was in danger. I passed over the note and pushed
past her into the kitchen. The kettle was boiling so I
made a pot of tea, not wanting to look at her face as she
read the note. I need not have bothered, there were no
hysterics of course. In fact she said nothing until I had
poured the tea and turned to face her.

"I'm flattered . . . says I'm pretty," she said brightly
and then frowned. "Or would you call that male
chauvinism? Perhaps I should feel insulted."

I ignored the banter. "Point is: what are we going to
do with you? You'll have to come down to Ardley and
live in sin for a week or two . . ."

"No chance," she said.

"Worried about your reputation?"

"About my job. I can't just walk out in the middle of a
series of projects. Besides, it seems a damn sight more

133

dangerous down there."

I smiled. "Perhaps you're right. But you will have to go away, Laura . . . somewhere. That's not a joke. You've never let the firm down before so you're entitled to put yourself first for once."

"All right, Matt, let's be serious. I *could* go, I suppose. But why should we just meekly do what they want? How do we know they're not bluffing?"

I shook my head. "They mean it. And even if I do as they want . . . if I chuck it in . . . which is what I should have done two weeks ago . . . I went down to Ardley to sell books, not play detective. If I chuck it in there's no guarantee they won't panic and do something nasty anyway. There's no point in trying to con ourselves into believing I can protect you, when I can hardly look after myself. They seem to be one jump ahead of me all the time . . ."

"It's not your fault," she protested. "It's just too much for one person to handle on his own. I don't want you to give up just because of me . . . really I don't but perhaps now you should pass it over to the police."

"But I found out more than the police did—why else are the bastards trying to shut me up? I can't for the life of me imagine how they found you. Frensham is the only one who knows about our relationship and since he recruited me he doesn't have a motive. I certainly didn't tell anyone I was coming here . . ."

She paused, the tea-cup at her lips. "Could you have been followed here earlier?"

I shrugged. "I wasn't aware of anyone. But then I wasn't really looking." I thought back over the day, starting with my telephone call, and then retraced those movements. The telephone call. That had to be the answer. As well as the break-in at the shop to start a fire, someone could have bugged the telephone at any time over the past week or two. Someone posing as a post office engineer checking lines would not have aroused

134

the suspicion of Charlie in my absence. There was no point in dwelling on *how* it might have been done—it was the obvious answer to their awareness of my movements. They probably knew about every contact I'd made and everything I had discussed openly on the telephone. I felt relieved at keeping back at least certain ideas and information from Inspector Murdoch. At least they hadn't seen my complete hand.

Laura poured us both a second cup of tea. "I'll do whatever you think is sensible. But don't let's panic."

I kissed her on the lips. "Play your cards right and I could get to be very fond of you."

She raised her eyebrows. "Now I know what it is you like about me—I'm compliant or just plain weak-kneed."

"What else? But irrespective of my motives and irrespective of what I decide to do about the investigation it makes sense for you to go away for a few days. Try to think of somewhere suitable but keep it to yourself for the moment. I don't know if they've got a plant in this room too. While we're talking more generally I'll look around."

Searching out hidden listening devices had been part of my basic training and I went through the living-room and bedroom systematically until I was satisfied that no-one had broken in. As I examined the phone I began to realise that a call to Inspector Murdoch was overdue. I was not prepared to take any more chances with Laura's safety.

It was just approaching midnight and I phoned Ardley police station to ask for the Inspector's home number, which was of course more complicated than I had expected. I told the duty sergeant that I had merely mislaid the number but it was not until after I had identified myself and then given Laura's telephone number ("if I was at home I wouldn't need to ring the station, I'd have the number in my address book") that

135

they relented.

A woman's voice answering the private number was momentarily disconcerting. I hadn't associated Murdoch with domesticity and the knowledge added a welcome note of humanity to the picture I had of him. It even made me think of apologising for troubling him so late. I then reported the threat and the circumstances in which it had been made. I asked if he would arrange for the Metropolitan police to put a watch on the flat. "She'll be leaving town for a few days—we haven't even decided where yet—but I'd feel happier if there was someone keeping an eye on the flat from the time I leave tomorrow."

Murdoch listened to my story without interruption and finally promised to contact the Met as soon as we had concluded our conversation. Then he sighed. "I wish you had been a little more forthcoming, Mr Coll. I can't believe that anyone would go to these lengths unless they were really worried about what you knew and what you even suspected. You obviously haven't told *me* everything . . ."

He still had the knack of making me feel like an ungrateful subordinate. "No, that's true," I conceded. "It's not a matter of holding back; more of not having the time to do everything that needs to be done. For example, I've been in London since this morning . . ."

"I know. I tried to contact you first thing. You see, *I* make the effort. Things are moving along. We've had some luck with the descriptions you gave us of the men in the stolen Jaguar."

My heart leapt. "That's fantastic! You've got them?"

"We know where to lay our hands on them so there's no urgency about bringing them in—especially as there have been other developments. But please stay in touch because sooner or later I'll need you for an identity parade. With any luck that'll only be a formality."

I was tempted to interrupt and mention my second

run-in with Bobby Miles but I suspected it would irritate him still more; that information could wait until we were face to face. Instead I congratulated him on what seemed like a break-through and asked about the other developments he had mentioned.

"Yes, rather more significant," he said with an unfamiliar note of enthusiasm in his dour voice. "Our friend Mr Heyman has come to an untimely end. He was found dead at the Erdington College library in Somerset when the caretaker opened up this morning. Seems he fell from the skylight trying to get away with a load of books."

I was stunned. The thought of all that restless energy suddenly cut off by one crushing fall was incongruous. I pictured his sensitive face frozen in death. Poor sod. I felt a sense of loss, almost sorrow, at the waste of such intelligence. Poor misguided devil. But even as the sentiment echoed in my mind I began to doubt the veracity of a report which could attribute his death to that unlikely manner. Heyman had been obsessional enough to have been involved in the book thefts but he was not a man of action. Steal a book in a moment of temptation perhaps but not break into a library through the skylight. It sounded crazy.

Murdoch whistled sharply down the telephone. "Are you still there?"

I grunted. "Sorry. I can't take it in. Are you sure it was him? He was a librarian, not a cat-burglar."

Murdoch sounded unimpressed. "That was my initial reaction but we can't argue with facts. We're still waiting for a pathologist's report; meanwhile there's no question he fell from the skylight and did himself a lot of mischief in the process."

"Would it be possible for me to see the body, d'you think?"

He hesitated. "I'm happy for you to see the photographs the local CID have taken. I can't really see

137

why you want to go all the way over to the mortuary . . . he's a bit of a mess."

The thought appalled me. I was suddenly ashamed of how I had bullied the little librarian but the way he had reacted strengthened my conviction he was not the sort of man to scamper over roof-tops and through sky-lights. I was not satisfied and said that I would appreciate a fuller account of Heyman's death when we met in the morning.

"Very well, Mr Coll," said Murdoch, "Now is the time for a full and frank *exchange*. You tell me what I need to know and I'll do my best to help you."

We arranged to meet at mid-day.

I told Laura what had happened but she had not known Heyman and her concern was for my distress. It was on a despondent and preoccupied note that we went to bed; so my apprehension at making love had been groundless. Laura fell asleep in my arms within minutes of going to bed and I lay awake for more than an hour, trying to formulate a plan of action. From now on I must call the play.

NINE

Laura was still asleep when I left the flat at 5 am. My own sleep had been intermittent and restless so I decided to get back to the West Country before the roads became congested. In a brief note I suggested that when she had made arrangements to stay with relatives or friends she should phone Frensham—from whom I would get the information later. I did not want to use my phone until the bug had been removed.

I had almost reached Ardley in time for breakfast when I decided to take a diversionary route to Oldham Park to see Caroline Berridge first. She was my only link with Heyman and I was not so infatuated that I did not remember my obligations. She should not have heard yet of the librarian's death so I would at least have the opportunity of assessing her reaction. I was confident she was not implicated in the robberies but suspected she might *know* more than she had admitted, probably out of a mistaken loyalty to Heyman.

I found Caroline and Lord Berridge at breakfast. Neither showed any surprise at my unexpected appearance at such an early hour. Her smile was warm but not unduly intimate but Henry Berridge was almost effusive. "Happy coincidence," he assured me. "I have to be in Ardley day after tomorrow—in the afternoon. Intended to take the opportunity to pop in and see those shooting books you mentioned."

"Please do. I'll try to rustle up a few interesting odds and ends."

Caroline asked if I would join them for breakfast but I was too much on edge to sit down to a meal. I settled instead for a cup of tea. Passing it to me, she said, "The last time you called I blithely assumed it was a social visit—and it wasn't. This time I'll assume it's the investigation . . ?"

Lord Berridge tried to look interested. "Got any news of *our* books?"

I shook my head. "It's not as though they were taken by some impoverished student who needed to dispose of them quickly for the money. I suspect we'll have to catch the culprits before we get the books back—the bulk of them anyway."

He nodded wisely. "Get your point. Is there any hope at all?"

"Of course. From just a couple of possible leads we've had quite a measure of success to date."

Caroline clapped her hands. "You *are* a dark horse, Matt. What have you found out?"

"Enough to provoke a couple of attacks on my life—if you'll excuse the dramatics."

I studied their faces. Caroline had flinched and her eyes were concerned—a reaction much the same as Laura's when I told her about Heyman's death. *That wasn't an act*, my alter ego crowed. *She really cares!* Her husband's reaction was quite the reverse. His eyes glittered with excitement. "I *say*, old boy. That's quite something. I don't know anything about books but if you need any help just say the word!"

He meant it and I was quite touched. I accepted that it was not my welfare that especially concerned him but the excitement of a scrap, but he could be a useful ally—if he could be controlled. Berridge was presumably a crack shot but he probably had few scruples about shooting first and asking questions later. He might easily find himself on a manslaughter charge.

I thanked him for his interest but declined the offer. "The police are involved now so we might find ourselves a little restricted—which is a pity because I've got a few scores to settle."

140

He looked disappointed. "Well, you know where I am if you need some back-up. Only too pleased. Not a great one for the administrative chores that keep me bogged down these days." He sighed and remembered his manners with a smile. "Would you please excuse me, old boy. If it's about the books Caroline's your man anyway."

I was relieved to see him go because it was Caroline's reaction to the news of Heyman's death I wanted. When he had gone Caroline offered me the option of staying where we were or going for a walk in the grounds. I wanted her in one spot so I suggested we move into the library.

The tiered ranks of leather bindings looked down on us, like justices at law, it seemed, sitting in judgement on Caroline's reaction to my news.

It was symbolic perhaps, rather than physical, yet the effect was heightened by the richness of the leather, dyed uniformly in a warm, blood red . . . projecting the ambience of a dignified benevolence, which I found vaguely reassuring. But in the midst of this brief hallucination I was aware for the first time of some new bindings, a small section done in a mottled green calf. They were housed in one corner and I suppose my eyes had not scanned that far in the past, when I had been more concerned with specific titles. Caroline confirmed my impression that these were contemporary bindings on old books. One hesitates to rebind and thus change the character of incunabula—or indeed mess about with any work of art—but one can inject fresh life into an otherwise undistinguished 17th or 18th century book and this is what seemed to have happened, judging by the titles.

I took a volume down from the shelf to examine it. The gilt decoration was heavily ornate and skilled but it was the quality of the leather and the way it had been worked that indicated the exceptional craftsmanship entailed. Perhaps unfairly one assumes that few modern craftsmen can reproduce the great standards of their predecessors but it was certainly uncommon to find bindings of such beauty.

She might have read my thoughts. "You're the book-seller. I'll give you two guesses as to where they were done . . ?"

I speculated. "There's some good stuff done in France, I'm told."

She was impressed. "You weren't misinformed. We were recommended to two binders, master craftsmen who don't charge the earth. I send them anything, other than simple repair jobs."

I would have liked to examine a few more but remembered why we were there. I took a deep breath and told her simply what Murdoch had told me, without warning, without embellishment, without any indication of my own feelings. My eyes never left her face as it registered a series of mixed emotions. My main impression was one of shock and I sensed that her initial thoughts were similar to mine.

Finally, in a hoarse voice, she replied. "I simply don't believe it."

"*I* didn't."

She looked as though she might burst into tears. "Has he been properly identified?"

I shrugged. "I didn't argue with Inspector Murdoch. He seemed sure enough and he's not the sort of person to jump to conclusions."

She shuddered.

"It means one of two things," I pointed out. "Either that he was involved much more than he admitted to me—he was actually part of a gang. Or . . . his death *wasn't* an accident."

"How could that be?"

"I shouldn't speculate without *all* the facts. But if he fell from a skylight, perhaps he was pushed. Murdoch

142

said he fell actually in the act of stealing. Well, I can see Heyman supervising but he'd need someone else to do the breaking and entering part, quite apart from humping the books . . ." I broke off, realising the pointlessness of speculation in the circumstances. "If someone was worried that Heyman's cover had been blown they might consider he'd become a liability."

"Do the police know if there was anyone else involved?" she asked. "Other clues—footprints, fingerprints, or whatever they look for."

I shrugged. "At the moment they're only concerned with him. What *I* want to know before I see Murdoch again is where *you* fit in."

Her eyes widened. "Me?"

"He phoned you the night I secured that confession. You gave me a vague story about just being friends but that's no longer good enough, Caroline. He must have told you more. I need to know."

Suddenly she shivered and pulled at the cardigan falling loosely over her shoulders in that rather pointless way that women seem to regard as fashionable. She looked so vulnerable that I moved closer and put my arms around her. She buried her face in my shoulder and clung to me, shivering. While it was not warm in the library—the central heating turned down to keep the books at an even temperature—she was not so much cold as frightened. She was on the verge of a confession if I handled the situation properly.

Tenderly I put her arms into the cardigan sleeves and adjusted it snugly. "Trust me . . ." I tried to push her to arms length so that she could see from my face that I was sincere but she held on tightly.

"I can't bear you to look at me," she said. "I'm too ashamed."

I squeezed her gently. "Well, we can't stay like this all morning. If Henry walks in he's bound to jump to the wrong conclusion."

Caroline pulled away and forced a smile although she kept her eyes down. "I'll be all right." She looked about her. "There's nowhere to sit down here," she complained with a faint grimace. "I must do something about that."

I pulled over a small stepladder and lifted her easily on to the wide top step, level with my waist. "Go on, tell me—from the beginning."

She shook her head. "I've told you that part—and I didn't lie. I could never lie to you, Matt. But I did leave things out. It really started once we had become friends. We were discussing our dreams one day. Mine, I remember, was to make a success of running Oldham Park—which didn't seem very likely at the time. His was to own a few very fine rare books, one of which happened to be in the Radford Library.

"We talked about realising those dreams. He said I would accomplish mine through my creativity in terms of ideas and hard work and he would his—by stealing the book from Radford. At first I thought he was joking . . . Of course he wasn't talking about robbery in the context of your investigation—for financial gain. He was talking of love. He looked at certain books in the way . . . well, in the way I would look at you, in other circumstances. He pointed out that the college library was insured and that he would put that substantial sum of money to good use on the college's behalf . . . the provision of books of greater interest and value to the college than the single copy he wanted for himself . . . in his lifetime. He had even thought of ways of returning it to the library when he died."

"So he did arrange his own break-in?"

"Yes, and I helped him indirectly . . . why do you think I was so ashamed?"

My heart sank but I said nothing.

"He was determined to go ahead and I'd given up trying to dissuade him. One day he said he had a

144

problem—where to hide the missing books? Obviously he couldn't use his own flat. He intended to take two or three other titles in case anyone was suspicious of the theft of a single one, especially one he was known to cherish. He suggested the best possible place was in another substantial library where they could be 'lost' for a while. When he looked at me I was absolutely adament. Friend or no friend, I couldn't be an accessory to a criminal act, but of course he worked on me. At the time our restoration fund was practically empty and we were so desperate for money we even contemplated selling the library, lock, stock and barrel. He seemed to *care* about the restoration fund. I shouldn't say 'seemed' because he *did* care. Anyone who really loves old books must have a feeling for antiquity of any sort and he was totally dedicated to preserving the past.

"So of course I weakened. He said he would carry out the theft irrespective of my co-operation but he wanted an opportunity to help Oldham Park, so . . . finally I agreed, in return for a gift of whatever he could raise on the sale of the unwanted books—2 or 3,000 pounds he estimated."

Caroline became upset at the recollection. She stopped and bit her lip hard. Then she turned her head away so that I couldn't see the tears welling up in her eyes. She climbed down from the step ladder and busied herself, straightening a row of books that were already quite straight, continuing her story as she worked. "For what its worth, and I'm not saying this in my defence, I didn't get anything after all. He brought the books here for a few days and took them away again without explanation. He was going to tell me all about it, he said, but never did. Perhaps it had something to do with the men he was frightened of . . ."

"But who were they?"

"I don't know and he said he didn't either." She

swallowed hard, produced a handkerchief from a sleeve and wiped her nose.

I was greatly relieved to discover there had been no financial gain. Although she was technically guilty of compounding a felony there was no evidence, other than what she had told me, and I saw no reason why anyone else should know. I told her. It was a mistake. She broke down.

"*I* know," she cried.

I couldn't bear to see her so upset. I took her in my arms again. This time she didn't attempt to hide. Her tear-stained face looked up at me for understanding and I couldn't resist kissing her. At long last her defences were down. I took advantage of her and, thank heaven, she responded. She returned my kisses with an ardour that belied her usual poise and that delicate beauty. Eventually she broke away. "Matt, I didn't want this to happen. We mustn't read anything into it. You're feeling sorry for me and perhaps I'm just grateful for a shoulder to cry on."

"That's not so," I told her firmly. "I knew I was in love with you long before. When you lectured me about the sanctity of marriage I tried to put it out of my mind. But although I suspected you shared my feelings—this is the first time you've behaved spontaneously."

She looked away. "Don't waste your time with me, Matt. Look what a mess I'm already in. I'm not worried for myself but if it gets out Henry will be ruined. What has he done to deserve that? He never suspected a thing."

I put a finger to her lips to halt the outburst. "Hush. It *won't* get out."

She kissed me lightly on the mouth. "But it's not fair to you. You're conducting an investigation—you can't just draw a veil over part of the case . . ."

"Why not? Heyman is dead. We'll never know what he was really up to. If he had this obsessive desire for certain books it might have been him who robbed Major Edwards over at Dorchester and even this library."

"Not ours, definitely not ours," she protested firmly. "He was my friend."

I shrugged. "Don't worry about the enquiry. I'm more concerned about us. What are we going to do . . ?"

She kissed me again, tenderly on the eyes, the nose and finally my mouth. "I can't leave Henry—or Oldham Park. It sounds crazy but they need me in equal measure. I honestly believe that the pressures would get on top of Henry and that might mean that ultimately he would have to sell. I couldn't do that to him. Not for what could merely be a rush of blood to the head."

"It's more than that . . . besides, what about *your* happiness?"

She smiled. "Same difference. I don't think my happiness is that important. Oldham Park will be a consolation, in the same way as the shop in Ardley will be yours. I know it means a lot to you."

"It isn't that important," I said, believing it.

"Then let's wait and see," she said. "I know it's not quite the same but we could see each other regularly. I'll come to the shop and if you don't think it's too sordid we'll make love whenever we get the chance . . ."

I laughed. "Too sordid? I'll settle for anything. Why couldn't we have met five years ago?"

She shook her head. "You wouldn't have liked me in those days. I was a very self-centred person."

I did not believe her. "When did this transformation take place?"

"After I got married. Responsibility. Doing something worthwhile. I didn't marry Henry for love. I can admit that now . . . to you. I married him because of pressure from my father who had a thing about security. My father was a gentleman by birth and you might say

147

by profession—and since to the true gentleman money is something only the poor concern themselves with he never had any. He must have been the only estate agent in the country who lived permanently on the verge of bankruptcy. The Berridge family to him represented respectability and security and, not being a business-man, he was incapable of realising Henry was no better off than him. The only difference in fact was Oldham Park which of course had some potential value if it could be made to work for it. So I grew up overnight and found something to live for. I may not love Henry but I've become very fond of him. And we're good friends."

"And your father?"

"He's dead now. Once I was safely married he had nothing much else to live for . . . I'm afraid I don't miss him."

I thought of Billy Lloyd's father but was reluctant to bring any of the Lloyd family into the conversation. I realised I was still jealous. Conscious that I would be late for my meeting with Murdoch, I told her I had to leave. She promised to telephone me later and kissed me good-bye, tenderly, as though we were parting for good. I left, walking on air.

I made my peace with Murdoch by telling him at once about the attempt to set fire to the shop—with me asleep upstairs. Although he was annoyed at my failure to report the incident he seemed to accept my excuse of being dazed and locking the stable door after the horse had bolted. "If they had been complete strangers I would have dialled 999—even though they were probably clean away—but I knew you were already onto Scarface so I thought there wasn't much to be gained." I admitted I had opened my own line of enquiry through the crime reporter on the Daily Chronicle but did not mention Billy Lloyd's connection.

Meanwhile I was keen to hear his report on Heyman's death. Murdoch produced a series of black-and-white photographs of a crumpled body, illustrating the injuries and its position in relation to the rest of the huge room. It was the little librarian all right but I was more fascinated by a haversack, from which a number of books had spilled, still strapped to his back. He noticed my interest and commented, "Must have been quite a weight. The pathologist's report indicates that he wasn't killed by the impact, as we initially thought. It *would* have killed him but seems he was already dead. Massive heart attack. Either caused by the strain of going up a rope ladder with that load on his back—or the fright of falling over backwards. Couldn't be more specific."

"Are you *sure* he was alone?"

"Not absolutely. Seems like it but the only un-resolved piece of evidence is a cupboard which was probably forced open by a tool of some sort . . . a jemmy in all probability . . . but there was nothing we could find that fits the bill."

"That's enough for me," I retorted. "I told you before he wasn't a cat-burglar but now you've seen the poor sod, seen what a physical wreck he was, why would he have attempted to carry all those books? Heyman was interested in quality, not quantity. He'd never have stolen ordinary academic books and even if his partners decided they were worth taking, why let *him* carry them?"

"Indeed," echoed Murdoch. "But then the whole relationship puzzles me. What does a college librarian, with apparently no interests outside his work, have in common with professional criminals . . ?"

I admitted I had already asked myself that question and failed to come up with an answer. "His motivation would have been the books, not the money," I speculated.

"And theirs the money, not the books," he inter-jected, "so if he hung on to the books what was in it for them? Surely there are simpler ways to make a dishonest living?"

I shrugged. "Perhaps he kept just the odd volume and they had the rest. He probably didn't have much of a say."

"But why get involved in the first place?"

"They might have approached him cold?"

He shook his head. "Too risky. Why pick on *him* unless they knew he was receptive?"

"He admitted he robbed the college library; perhaps they found out and blackmailed him?"

"How would they know unless someone told them?"

The question worried me. Heyman had said Caroline was his only confidante. I dismissed the thought. She was even less likely than him to cross the path of criminals. There may well have been an intermediary but not her. I told Murdoch I was baffled.

Obviously he was not terribly bothered. "As I told you before, Mr Coll, I'm more interested in known criminals. If your speculation is correct then we're dealing with murder: the assumption being that they knew we were on to him. The question is, who were they? No ordinary men—they'd have to be exceptionally ruthless."

"Why don't you start with Scarface? They don't come any nastier."

"Why don't I? Don't disappear this time, Mr Coll. I'll need you in the next day or so. When the Met have detained our friend Miles I'll send someone up to fetch him, then we'll put him in a line-up. He certainly won't talk unless he sees we've got a watertight case."

"Watertight is what it better be—after my experience in the river."

He smiled thinly. "Meanwhile, give us a description of his other companions and we'll try to lay our hands on them too."

It was late afternoon when I got back to the shop to be

greeted by a glowing Charlie Appleton announcing our best weekday's trading since the business had begun. Coming on top of the breakthrough in my relationship with Caroline, I felt rejuvenated, happier than I had been in months. The mood turned to elation later with a phone call from the housekeeper at Oldham Park enquiring if I was available the following evening to join Lord and Lady Berridge for dinner . . .

TEN

The euphoria was shortlived. Only a few hours earlier I had been scared out of my wits by the threat to Laura; by telling her to leave the flat and asking for a police surveillance I had blithely assumed the danger would go away. I'd forgotten I was dealing with professionals. Next morning I was awakened by the phone call that shattered my complacency. The voice was muffled or disguised but the message was clear enough and my stomach lurched, throwing my brain off-balance. "Who's that . . ?" I enquired stupidly.

He chuckled. "A friend. A friend who wants to do you a favour. But first you've got to *prove* you care what happens to your girl-friend . . ."

"There's nothing to prove," I protested.

"We've got to know for certain that you've learned your lesson—and laid off; not just *kidding*."

"How do I know *you're* not kidding?" I thought wildly of keeping him talking so that someone could trace the call, except of course that there wasn't a 'someone'.

Then her voice was on the line, as cool and unflustered as I might have expected. "Don't worry about me, Matt—I'm all right."

"Laura . . ." I began.

But the man returned. "That'll do. Just so you know we're not bluffing. And if you don't chuck it *today*, someone is going to be doodling on that pretty face of hers with a razor."

I struggled to stay calm. "What proof is there you'll keep your word? I'll drop the investigation from this moment but how can I believe *you*?"

152

"You don't have a choice. But this isn't a bloody hotel. We want her off our hands as soon as possible. Either way she'll have to stay for about a week. That's all we need—a few more days without any bother . . ."

I didn't trust him but he was right—I had no choice. "Let me speak to her then," I said.

Laura came to the phone. She was about to reassure me but I interrupted her impatiently. "Did you hear all that . . ?"

"Yes."

"Well, we're not taking any chances. I'm phoning Frensham now to resign—he'll understand. But do you think you can hang on for a few days?"

"Matt, you can't give up now . . ."

I felt choked although I wouldn't like to say whether it was emotion or irritation; she had no right to be so considerate. But before I could think of a suitably encouraging reply the man had cut in. "Be a good boy now. We'll be in touch." He put the phone down.

I replaced the receiver automatically, my thoughts angry and confused; angry at myself for not *doing* more to protect Laura and angry at the police. I should have rung Frensham without delay but I had a bloody-minded desire to shatter Inspector Murdoch's smugness. He was constantly reminding me about stepping out of line and yet someone at his end had presumably slipped up. Concern for Laura gnawed away at my conscience until I felt I had to vent my speen on someone.

Murdoch was suitably humbled by the news and in the face of his honesty I had to come down to earth. I realised of course that the responsibility had been with the London police and there seemed little point in blaming him. Apparently the Met had promised to keep Laura's flat under surveillance and to keep an eye on her as far as possible. He volunteered to find out what had gone wrong.

When I had reported my discussion with one of the kidnappers and my promise to forget the enquiry he sounded sympathetic. "That's probably very wise, Mr Coll, although I'm glad you didn't panic and try to conceal the news from us."

"I said I'd stop investigating the thefts and I will," I pointed out. "But since I wouldn't trust them to keep their side of the bargain we've got to find Laura as soon as possible."

"You're right," he conceded. "And it's fortunate you've phoned because *I* have some news for *you*. A letter from Heyman. I picked it up from his solicitors . . . one of those 'only to be opened in the event of my death' letters. It's addressed to you but I knew you'd have no objection to me opening it, especially as it might have contained a confession. No such luck, I'm afraid."

"Nothing?"

"He was involved all right but only a small cog. Still, he does give us a lead. I'd like your opinion . . ."

Having asked him to read it out, I heard the rustle of paper and Murdoch, muttering or reading under his breath. "I'll skip over the first couple of pages," he eventually announced. "It's a bit like eavesdropping on a private conversation, a sort of unburdening of the soul. Talks of man's obligation to preserve his heritage and having betrayed that trust . . . You can read all that at your leisure. The meat is contained in just a couple of paragraphs. I'll read that:

'I'm a fool, not a crook. In a moment of weakness, thinking I was helping a friend, I did something dishonest. If one plays with fire, one must expect to get burned. Since then I've had to do what they demanded—partly blackmail, but partly to continue protecting my friend, who has much more to lose

154

than me.

'If anything should happen to me, the only way I can still help this person is to speak out and hope that you can stop them. I don't know who they are. All I had to do was to send a list of books and their locations once a month to a post office box number. I've never seen any of them, but I had a telephone call yesterday. For some reason they want me to go with them to the Erdington library next week. God knows why.

'Having said I would speak out there's very little to speak out about. The only *half* clue I can offer is a strange conversation a week or so ago with Billy Lloyd, the city businessman. We met socially and I was flattered by his attention, but even at the time I was puzzled—it was almost a third degree. Later I was also conscious of him staring at me . . .'

Inspector Murdoch sighed. "There's some more personal stuff but nothing of value to our enquiries. The first thing that struck me is that Lloyd comes from London and the post office box number Heyman mentioned was in London. What do you think?

I hesitated. If I was completely frank Murdoch might feel he had enough to go on and elbow me out of the way. I wanted to keep my head start. "Very interesting," I countered. "I'd like to put the proposition to Mr Lloyd."

He grunted. "You're forgetting you've just resigned the case. Meanwhile, what about the mysterious friend Heyman says he was trying to protect?

My heart sank and I reintroduced the topic of Lloyd to distract his attention from Caroline, assuring myself he would only be confused. "I think Lloyd might even have something to do with Miss Cottingham's disappearance . . ."

Murdoch snorted. "That's dangerous talk. Mr Lloyd

is an ostensibly respectable businessman—and a rich one. I can't see him speculating his petty cash on a few stolen books."

It would have been splitting hairs to disagree but I reported the link between Miles and Lloyd. "He denied it," I conceded, "but I've seen a photograph taken by the Daily Chronicle which proves Miles was working for him at one stage as a bodyguard. It was that which first made me suspicious. I met Lloyd through Lord Berridge—he's got financial interests in Oldham Park—and he got to hear what I was doing. I thought at first it might be poor Heyman but only the other day I found someone had bugged my phone . . ."

". . . and you didn't tell me?"

"I haven't had a moment. It was all too sophisticated for our Mr Miles so my thoughts returned to Lloyd. Just thoughts, but now we've got Heyman's input."

"Perhaps it's time for me to have a chat with him . . ."

I begged him for just 36 hours to chase up a couple of leads.

"What leads?" he replied. "I thought you'd told me everything?"

"Not even leads—just hunches. I'll report back tomorrow."

He hesitated for a moment and then agreed, with a schoolmasterish proviso that I behaved myself.

My fears about finding a way to trap Lloyd were alleviated when I phoned to make an appointment and learned that he had been invited to join us for dinner at the Berridges' that evening. In my concern for Laura I had actually forgotten about it and for a moment I wondered why he had been asked. But it saved me a visit to London and he wouldn't have the advantage of being on his own territory. With that resolved I phoned Frensham.

It transpired that the dinner was Caroline's way of putting her cards on the table. Lord Berridge's gratitude at my suggestion of not making her "confession" public was almost emotional. Over the meal I listened with only half an ear to the pleasantries and Berridge's long discourse on the cost of running Oldham Park; I was preoccupied with trying to catch out Lloyd.

Eventually I interrupted almost rudely to announce my news—I was stopping the investigation. Berridge and Caroline were obviously stunned and even Lloyd looked surprised.

"You're not going to let them get off scot-free?" Berridge demanded.

I told him I had no choice. "They've threatened a friend in London."

He shook his head sadly. "They don't miss a trick."

"What about asking the police for protection?" suggested Lloyd.

"It's not worth the risk," I said.

"I'm inclined to agree," replied Lloyd. "It's one thing when there's only ourselves to think about. Not the same when there's someone else involved. With you living down here there's no way you can protect her." My sharp reaction showed on my face but he recovered himself. "I say 'her' because I assume Matt has a beautiful woman tucked away somewhere. Am I right?"

Conscious of the look of surprise on Caroline's face, I nodded. "Partially right. I'd underline the word 'friend'. Probably the only true friend I have in London . . . which is why they picked on her."

He nodded complacently. But I was elated. He had slipped up at last. That had been no inspired guess or assumption. He *knew*.

I was too excited by Lloyd's slip to enjoy the rest of the meal. I managed to put on an act but luckily Lloyd tended to dominate the conversation so I was able to daydream for long spells. My heart leapt when Caroline asked him over coffee if he would drive back to London or stay the night and he accepted their offer of a guest bedroom. I was determined to make use of his absence.

Despite eight drugged hours the previous night I was desperately short of sleep and probably in no condition to drive to London and then break into a house I had not reconnoitred for that purpose. Even though the adrenalin temporarily recharged my batteries the monotony of the long drive in the dark began to tap that spare energy and I was soon feeling drowsy. After a couple of minor lapses of concentration, which might have been dangerous had there been any traffic about, I consciously slowed the pace. I had left Oldham Park a little after midnight and if I arrived at Lloyd's house in just over two hours I would have ample time before he or his staff turned up in the morning. The house was detached and reasonably secluded. Unless there was an alarm system I was not concerned about finding a way in although I was certainly not dressed for the job if there was any climbing to do. Fortunately there was a pair of thin leather gloves in the car.

The house was in darkness. I assumed it was empty and although the thought did occur to me that Lloyd might have a woman friend in residence I decided it was unlikely. I parked the car in a side road, emptied my pockets of anything that could drop out and walked back to the house.

The street was deserted. Although I was reasonably confident everyone was asleep I ignored the front of the house. The back however was equally overlooked by a tall block of flats so, opting for caution, I was restricted to the side. There were no windows on the ground floor but four above—although only one was not secured. About 25 feet from the ground, it was a single metal-framed casement window opening outwards from what I guessed was the bathroom.

The only means of access was a drainpipe which ran up the side of the building a distance of about six feet from the edge of the window sill. It wasn't easy but I was tempted by the slight opening in the window. The pipe itself was no problem and, having donned the driving gloves to protect my hands against the brickwork, I shinned up it with remarkably little effort, considering I was out of practice.

It was when I reached the level of the window that the real test began. With my right hand I clung to the drainpipe, gripping it between my legs, and gradually eased my body against the face of the wall, reaching with the fingertips of my left hand for the sill. Even in that spreadeagled position I was about a foot away—a formidable distance to bridge in the circumstances. But I could not afford to hesitate. I lifted my feet until I was practically squatting against the wall, braced my thighs, pushed hard against the pipe and leapt sideways for the sill. I managed to cover the gap but my clutching fingers could not retain their precarious hold and I fell.

In mid-air I managed to twist my body round so that I was no longer facing the wall and could judge my landing more easily. At the moment of impact I rolled over and got to my feet none the worse, except for a throbbing pain in the fingers of my left hand. With a fairly good idea of how my error of judgement could be rectified I climbed up again. This time I contrived to jump outwards, away from the wall, so that the movement was less restricted, and then at the peak of my impetus grabbed for the sill and held fast. Then I quickly brought over my right arm to share the strain. Gradually transferring my weight to the right, I put the other hand inside the window, open just a few inches, and loosened the metal bar which controlled the window's movement. Then with the same hand I swung the casement outwards over my lowered head. All I had to do now was to gain a better grip on the inside of the window with my left hand, shift my right over too and haul myself up and through.

Only when I was inside the bathroom did I notice the tremendous strain I had imposed on my arms. Feeling twice their size, they began to tremble violently, so that I had to wait for several minutes until they had recovered. Once inside however—where to start? I dismissed Lloyd's office on the ground floor because there were probably few places to which his private secretary did not have access and I doubted whether he allowed her to become aware of any extra-mural criminal activity. I started instead with his bedroom and, more by luck than judgement, found a wall-safe behind the solitary framed print facing the bed. The picture was an American-style fight scene, looking like a giant blow-up of the old Ring magazine front cover, although I had to admit it was riveting. At the same time it was a singularly unimaginative place to conceal a safe.

As I took the frame down my heart sank. Opening relatively simple safes had been part of my training in the service but it had been years since I had any practice. It was not a sophisticated type although still formidable enough to unnerve me. The only thing in my favour was time. The safe was controlled by a combination and to crack it I needed just that and luck. Since it was going to be a long job I decided to work in relative comfort so I drew the curtains and switched on the light. Before tackling the combination I examined the surrounding area in the faint hope that Lloyd had scratched the number; I had been lucky in the past. However this time I had to work hard for my incriminating documents—if indeed they even existed. It seemed incredibly humid and in my concentration I began to sweat, the scattered globules of water gradually becoming a small torrent. I became edgy, wondering if I was not wasting my time and whether my action was not influenced by personal dislike and jealousy.

The time dragged but at the back of my mind I realised I would eventually crack the combination. More often than not the series of digits conformed to a limited number of variations on a set formula and a trained person was usually capable of applying this knowledge to what he knew of the owner and the type of combination he might employ; it was sometimes merely a question of running through the possible variations until one found the right one.

Then with tantalising suddenness the door swung open with a gentle click—as though it had been teasing me. Inside the view was hardly promising—only a handful of papers. I removed them systematically. The first sheaf were share certificates and apparently innocuous business papers which seemed to belong more to the office safe if there was one. I wondered why they were even here and whether they might be of any interest to the City Fraud squad; they meant nothing to me. There were letters, equally meaningless, whose senders were unknown to me. And finally three large envelopes.

In one was an imposing selection of letterheads on virgin paper—the House of Commons and House of Lords were both represented—which I imagined might be used by Lloyd for faking or forging business letters.

The second contained a smaller envelope with a French stamp postmarked "Marseille". Inside was a handwritten note, in French, which meant little to me, except that it was addressed to Lloyd and signed "Pierre". It was dated about three months earlier but, try as I might to get some overall impression, my grammar school French was not up to it. Tantalisingly, odd words or phrases would pop up for identification but my triumph was always short-lived. I should have

161

conceded defeat but I continued to stare obstinately at the letter, as though I needed to memorise it. I had a feeling it was significant, but *only* a feeling, so there seemed little point in taking it with me. I put it on one side for the moment and picked up the third.

This time I was fortunate, pulling out something far more sinister—a sheaf of invoices, seventy to one hundred years old, from booksellers and auction houses. The sales itemised were in the main for undistinguished books and it occurred to me immediately that by eradicating the ink, which was quite simple, the bills could be used for faking sales records and giving an alternative history for books that had been stolen . . . indeed how the thieves might produce a false provenance. I was still marvelling at my good fortune when I heard a discreet cough. I froze and knew without turning round that I had been discovered. The only questions were—by whom and whether there was a chance for me to escape. I turned slowly.

Lloyd was leaning in the doorway, as cool as ever. "Looking for something, sweetheart?" he lisped in a passable imitation of Humphrey Bogart.

The initial anger at my carelessness subsided and I smiled at his understandable complacency. I held up the envelope. "I had a sneaking suspicion you were involved in some way," I said. "There was no evidence though and I still can't see *why*—you don't need the money . . ."

"Exactly. I don't *want* the money—or the books. I don't even want what *you* want—Caroline. I've come to the conclusion you must be a bit of a nutcase."

I shook my head. "I'm not interested in motive. My suspicion of you was purely instinctive. Someone's been watching me very closely—someone with brains, enough at least to stay one step ahead of me all along. You slipped up over the threat to Laura. When you said

162

you were staying the night at Oldham Park I thought I'd see what I might find here. Why *did* you come back, by the way?"

He laughed. "Your preoccupation through dinner. Normally you watch Caroline like a hawk but for once you kept staring at me. Then you dashed off without the usual pleasantries. So I wondered what the hurry was. I gave you time to get back to Ardley and when there was no reply to my phone call I gambled that you'd come here. My car is pretty fast as you can imagine."

"I can."

"Tell me, what is the difference between people who break into shops or libraries to steal—and people who break into private premises for the same purpose?"

"I'd say a great difference—principally of motive. Their motive is personal gain; mine to uncover information that benefits the community as a whole, not just myself."

"What does that mean—'community as a whole'? A few affluent booksellers and even richer libraries?"

"Now who's trying to justify himself?"

He frowned. "You're trying my patience, Coll. We'll see what the police think about your bravado." He walked past me to the telephone and picked up the receiver.

I sat down in one of those huge leather swivel chairs. I can never understand why people have easy-chairs in a bedroom, hardly a place for sitting about—except perhaps in a hotel.

Lloyd paused with his first finger in the 9. "What am I doing?" he suddenly asked. "I can't waste my time giving evidence at a petty little court case—why don't I just toss you out on your ear?"

I shrugged. "Decisions. You've got a problem, either way. Ring the police and I'll simply tell Inspector Murdoch, who's working on the case, *why* I broke in—and show him these old invoices. It wouldn't

163

exactly excuse my conduct in their eyes but he'd be very interested. He might also have a word with the boys in the fraud squad.

"On the other hand, tossing me out might not be as easy as you think. I wouldn't want your past glories to lull you into a sense of false security."

This time the calculated insult penetrated that composure. He put the phone down. "You've saved me the bother of deciding."

Watching him, tight-lipped and breathing deeply in an effort to control his temper, my stomach turned over. He reminded me of a bull pawing the ground before the charge and I realised there was a gulf between even hard men like Miles and a professional fighter, especially one who outweighed me by at least a stone. At his peak Lloyd had scaled around 175 lbs but good living had added another 30 lbs and very little of that seemed to be fat. I tried a little more psychology.

"I want it understood that I didn't come looking for a fight so you're going into this with your eyes open. You've been warned."

He was beginning to blow his top. "Get out of that bloody chair, you cheeky sod."

"Not until I have your word—you won't try to sue me later for assault. You're bound to come off worst because, unlike you, I wasn't trained under Marquess of Queensbury rules. I went to a dirty school—perhaps the best and dirtiest in the country."

I had calculated on unnerving him—he must have realised that I could have been speaking the truth—but he was too angry to absorb the implications. "I said, get out of the chair. I've forgotten the Marquess of Queensbury rules anyway."

"You might have been up to it once," I said mockingly, "but not with that great paunch . . ."

His anger finally spilled over. Not prepared to wait any longer for me to "square up", he charged forward to

164

haul me out of the chair. But as he approached I suddenly swivelled round so that he collided with the high back as I jumped clear. In mid-air I chopped down with the edge of my right hand against the back of his neck. I put a considerable weight behind the chop as he rushed by and had my timing been a fraction better he might have gone down. But the neck muscles were powerful and absorbed the impact without any noticeable effect.

Now we faced each other squarely and with the element of surprise lost I decided to let him commit himself and counter. It was a mistake because my co-ordination was unpredictable. I responded prematurely to a feint with his right fist and moved inside and on to a left hook which caught me high on the head. Considering that Lloyd was a heavy puncher and I had maximised the effect by meeting it halfway, I reckoned I was lucky not to have been decapitated. As it was, my head seemed to explode; my knees turned to water and I clutched desperately at him for support. I stuck to him tight as a clam while he tried to pummel me free. Dazed though I was I summoned my reserves of strength and managed to stand up sharply, aiming my head like a battering ram at the underside of his jaw. The pain in my head, already throbbing, was intense but I had the satisfaction of hearing him grunt with pain and step back.

On reflection, I should have gone for his legs but the sight of him flexing his jaw gingerly tempted me into measuring the injured zone for a left hook. I let go a pretty snappy hook but he blocked it instinctively with his guard and countered with a blow to my chest. Again I felt as though I had walked into a wall and realised that a few more like that around the head and I would end up in hospital. As he rushed in to follow up his advantage I kicked him in the groin and he staggered. I did the same with the other foot and he collapsed to his knees.

Mentally I gave a huge sigh of relief. I hadn't relished the prospect of mixing it with Lloyd for much longer. I moved nearer. A final boot in his stomach would finish him. As I swung my foot back he suddenly came to life, grabbed at my other leg and pulled me off balance. As I fell back I could see his face contorted with pain at the effort. There was no question of Lloyd's throwing in the towel; I'd have to batter him unconscious. He held on to my foot and twisted so that I had to follow the direction of its momentum and on to my stomach. Still holding on to my shoe, he scrambled towards me and brought his knees down on the small of my back.

For a crazy moment I half hoped he was going to clap me into a wrestling hold, in which I would have the chance of a rest and time to think of my next move. I certainly hadn't used my brains so far. But it was a forlorn hope. He let go of my foot to punch me about the head and I suddenly had a terrible mental picture of my battered head flying off and rolling about the room. Even as I was praying for unconsciousness—he had hit me three times and I couldn't understand how I could remain conscious—I realised that to get a better leverage he was no longer bothering to hold me down and with a tremendous effort I managed to throw him off. As we sprawled in different directions I lashed out with my foot and caught him in the face.

Whether it was a question of dignity or whether we were just more circumspect, we made no attempt to wrestle on the ground. Instead we climbed slowly to our feet before squaring up again. The fight had so far lasted only a few minutes but I was feeling exhausted—and he looked as though he was in a similar state. From now on it seemed as though it was going to be a battle of wills. We circled each other warily and he threw a left hook which I saw in time enough to block—or perhaps it was merely that the punch was slower? Instead of countering immediately I hesitated before trying one of my

166

own, which he evaded with little fuss, and then suddenly we were throwing punches like windmills or pub brawlers rather than trained fighters. Most scythed through the air with a tremendous expenditure of energy but little effect other than exhaust the persons throwing them. The blows became more ponderous and our breathing more stertorous but no-one got on top. Then one of my punches caught him over the right eye, which began to puff up, giving me considerable satisfaction; I wondered how he would explain that to his business associates. But the satisfaction was short-lived as I felt my nose apparently explode and vomit blood.

Our movements were becoming more and more uncoordinated and I was conscious of my heart pounding furiously. I wished desperately that he would lie down or concede and deeper down wondered whether I would lose face by doing so myself. Incredibly my wish was granted. He suddenly broke off, walked to the dressing-table mirror and examined his swollen eye. I could have attacked him from behind but I was too dispirited to continue and waited with bated breath for him to face me again. To my relief he smiled.

"We must be mad. What d'you say we call it a draw?"

I nodded. "Either that or we'll end up at the mortuary."

"Fine. Forgive me if I don't see you out. I want to put a compress on my eye."

I looked down at the documents from the safe, now spread out on the bed, and longingly at the large envelope with the old sales invoices. Our eyes met and he shook his head.

"They're not going anywhere," he said, "unless you want to resume our little bundle. It's hardly worth it."

I turned to go, feeling a little foolish at the way the situation had been resolved.

"Just a minute," he demanded, picking up the phone and dialling. Not taking his eyes off me, he spoke softly into the phone. "Let her go!" There was a momentary flash of anger in his expression at what must have been a protest. "I'll take the responsibility." He put down the receiver and smiled. "It wasn't my idea. At least you won't be going empty-handed."

I was puzzled. "You've just given me further proof that you're in with them."

He shook his head. "Your word against mine."

I nodded and left.

ELEVEN

I waited outside Laura's flat for her to return. My swollen nose in the driving mirror reflected the irony of my earlier lies; surely they had merely anticipated events, since now I probably *would* need a check-up. My inspection was interrupted by a car's pulling into the kerb in front of me, depositing Laura on the pavement and racing off. The street lighting was bad so I was unable to make out the occupants; nor was my sluggish brain able to record the licence number.

Laura stood for a moment, confused, and then spotted me getting out of the car. Typically her recent experiences were pushed to one side the moment she saw my battered face and I was obliged to give an edited account of what had happened to me. We compared notes, dipping liberally into a bottle of whisky. It seemed she had been well treated but could remember nothing of significance; obviously they did not let her know where she was being held or let her see them.

Annoyed with herself, she admitted having made it easy for them to trace her. Deciding to stay with a friend in Surrey, Laura had—thinking that her office might need her urgently—instructed the telephone exchange to refer calls to the temporary number. And so next day she received an invitation to the theatre and dinner with Frensham. The appointment was made by an efficient-sounding secretary and since the site was at the National Theatre and she intended to drive there and straight back it seemed harmless enough.

I phoned Ardley police and asked for a message about Laura's release to be conveyed to Murdoch and his contacts in the Met. I was on the point of adding that I

169

would be back in the shop the following afternoon when I looked at my watch and corrected myself . . . it was already 4 am.

We were desperately tired but Laura felt the need for a hot bath, while I bathed my nose and examined the damage carefully. A rudimentary knowledge of first aid convinced me it was merely swollen; the bone seemed to be in one piece. Relief made way for exhaustion. Oblivious of the most desirable woman only a few feet away, I could think only of sleep. I barely remember climbing into bed; only of being awakened with a cup of tea by Laura, announcing that it was mid-day, and was I "interested" in getting up? As I responded my whole body felt as though it had been flattened by a steam-roller—and I wondered how I was going to move about without a couple of sticks.

I groaned. "I feel as though I've been raped by a rhinoceros."

She snorted. "The things you country boys do for kicks!"

I sipped at the tea which was more welcome than any alcohol could have been. Not only did it begin to restore my morale but the heat seemed to have the effect of oiling badly worn joints. I decided to see what effect a hot bath might have and gingerly climbed out of bed.

Laura's expression was concerned. "An X-ray might not be a bad idea."

"Nothing broken," I insisted but beginning to doubt it. "Just bruising . . . pretty extensive and pretty bad. Don't worry, I'll get a check-up if it doesn't feel any better later in the day."

"You might stay in bed, at least."

"I've got a customer coming in this afternoon. Nothing Charlie couldn't handle better than me but I promised to see him."

The bath did help. The aches and bruises remained but the stiffness eased so that I felt more mobile

170

although exceptionally delicate. A couple of whiskies put a little pep into the scrambled eggs Laura had prepared. Then I phoned Charlie and asked him to gather a mixed bag of books on guns and hunting for Henry Berridge.

I used the drive to Ardley to reflect on the inconsistencies of the case. My mind went down the list of stolen books committed to memory and it suddenly occurred to me that I had been almost obsessed with the books at the top end of the market; maybe something to do with the possible evidence of forged provenance. Yet on Frensham's last list relatively few were really valuable—some almost ordinary. I wondered if it represented a new pattern; if that could be significant. Logically, with the trade on its guard, rare books were now more carefully protected; in any case, the number of sales outlets at those prices was limited. Yet why were they even bothering with books worth about a tenner a time, easier to lift singly during normal hours?

Berridge had not yet arrived so I gave Charlie the remainder of the afternoon off.

From his initial diffidence I formed the impression that Berridge had probably never bought a book in his life. I suspect his visit was partly a genuine interest in the subject and partly because of an obligation he felt he owed to a local tradesman who "played the game". He did a double-take at my swollen nose but as a gentleman offered no comment. He was fascinated by the books and it was apparent I had found a new and regular customer. Obviously not a reading man—I doubted whether he had ever read a novel or indeed anything other than the various field sports magazines—and when he glanced through my selected stock it was the illustrated books that first captured his attention. Gradually his interest in the subject and the views of fellow enthusiasts from past generations reached an untapped core of enthusiasm. His eyes began to

171

sparkle—or, to be more accurate, glitter—and he spent twenty minutes browsing through a dozen books before announcing that he would take them all.

"Will you take a cheque?" he enquired ingenuously.

I laughed at his frankness. "Perhaps I should insist on a guarantee . . . what about Billy Lloyd?"

"By all means. Except that you might lose a sale. He'd suggest there were better things I could do with my money."

"I thought he shared your interest in guns and hunting?"

He was surprised. "Who told you that? Billy is interested in hand-guns, admittedly. Target shooting or whatever they call it. He's not a hunting man."

"But I thought he goes shooting with you from time to time?"

Berridge appeared embarrassed. "Lloyd . . . Billy, is a business advisor—the best. Sometimes one has to socialise with one's business associations. He's not really our sort of person. Caroline tends to be nice to him but then she's pleasant to everyone."

Bloody snob, I thought. *It wouldn't occur to you to be jealous unless the man was from your own social circle. Well, in the circumstances, it makes it easier for me* . . . I decided there was no point in telling him yet about Lloyd's involvement in the robberies but the memory of those old sales invoices reminded me that I wanted his assistance. "It was your great-grandfather who started the library."

"No. My great-great-grandfather."

"Oh yes. I believe he kept some sort of diary relating to his interest in books?"

"Not a diary. Don't know where you get that impression. A book or whatever you call it. A book-keeping record of his purchases; most of them."

"That's right," I agreed, "Caroline offered to show it to me but I was a bit offhand at the time. I've since

172

realised that there must be some material that would assist the ABA in another matter. Could I arrange to take a look?"

"Of course. Why don't you phone my wife?"

That was the last thing I wanted to do. "I couldn't face her now," I replied with the confidence born of a half-truth. "I'd be happy to pop in some time although perhaps I could even check certain points on the phone?"

He shrugged. "Don't see why not. What sort of things?"

I considered. "When he started, for example. Exactly when. When he bought specific titles. That sort of information makes a contribution to the provenance of an important book. Just a question of checking details."

Lord Berridge had been my only customer during the early part of the afternoon so I looked up instinctively when the door-bell sounded. I found myself staring into the smiling face of Bobby Miles and his companions from the night of the attempted arson. Their appearance was so unexpected I was momentarily stunned although again I had time to wonder inconsequentially where the young Jaguar driver was. "Good afternoon, sir," Miles announced cheerfully. "We've come about a reported gas leak. I'm afraid you'll have to close up for a short while while we just have a look at your pipes . . ."

I considered calling his bluff but the last thing I wanted in my present battered state was a fight, for which they had probably come prepared—especially in the shop where some books might get damaged. Even if Berridge joined in we wouldn't come through unscathed. On the other hand we might do better with an element of surprise. I took the cheque from Berridge and put it in the cash till.

"Thanks very much, sir," I announced, addressing

him as a stranger. "You'll find those books on ancient Rome in the shed at the back—on the floor next to the door. Luckily you can get out that way, since we seem to be shutting the shop for a while."

For a moment he regarded me as though I was mad but since he had his back to the newcomers they could not have seen that expression. Then the penny dropped and he realised something was wrong. "You'll give me a call in the next month or so when the others come in?" he responded.

"I'll do my best, sir," I replied, pointing through the door at the back. As he followed the direction of my pointing finger I hoped he would do something useful— preferably call the police and hurry back.

As he disappeared Miles signalled to the youth to pull down the front door blind and lock the door, before addressing me happily. "Well now, Mr Coll . . . day of reckoning."

I regarded him with loathing. "I'm surprised you had the nerve to come back after the beating I gave you last time . . ?"

He refused to take offence. "Life's full of surprises. You see, I reckon you took unfair advantage of me the other night. Playing around with dangerous weapons— could have done me a serious mischief. If I'd known I'd have come with a shooter, wouldn't I?"

"What do you want?" I demanded.

"You, squire. This time we're not messing about. We're taking you out."

"What, in broad daylight and in the middle of the High Street?"

"High Street?" he echoed with a laugh. His companions joined in.

"What I mean is—I reported your earlier cock-ups to the police. And they've already identified you. They'll have circulated your description round here."

He nodded. "I had a tip-off they was looking for me.

174

But I'm currently of 'no fixed abode', which is a bit of a problem for them. This afternoon I'm at a mate's house—playing cards with witnesses—so they can't blame me if some yobbos come in to rob the till and bash you over the head in the process—can they?"

I studied him for a second, trying to penetrate his evil brain, and hazarded a guess. "So you're the one who killed Heyman?"

"The little professor?" he enquired innocently. "What, me? Never! He fell off a rope ladder at some library. Nicking books he was. Should have kept his nose clean, shouldn't he?"

I asked another question to distract him. "How did you know that he'd spoken to me?" My tone was interested, my manner relaxed as I strolled from behind the counter, but as he opened his mouth to answer I thrust the stiffly extended fingers of my left hand at his eyes. The half formed words contorted into a scream of pain. Fingers, stiff as metal rods, speared into his face on either side of the nose, high up, and dislodged the eyeballs. His hands reached up involuntarily and as they found the sockets with eyeballs now hanging over the lower eyelids retreated urgently in terror and revulsion.

His companions stood transfixed until, half in fear of what I might do to them next and half in anger at the horror that had been perpetrated on Miles, they rushed towards me. The nearer was the older, more powerful man and I dodged behind a bookcase and tipped it over at his approach. The books cascaded over him; he lost his balance and was trapped beneath the heavy metal frame. The noise was deafening but even so I was conscious of a sound at the other end of the shop and looked up in time to see Lord Berridge jump on the youth—who surrendered without a struggle. Berridge gave him a clubbing punch for good measure and the youngster burst into tears.

175

The battle was over; it had lasted no more than ten seconds.

I turned first to Miles who was moaning softly. "For Chrissake, help me. Get me to a doctor," he appealed.

I felt no sympathy for him. Indeed I was tempted to straighten the mess before ringing for an ambulance but at that moment there was a rattle at the shop door and a demand to "Open up—police!"

I climbed over the pile of books, ignoring the thug struggling fruitlessly to extricate himself, and pushed up the blind before unlocking the door. Two police-men—one very tall and fair, the other stocky and bearded—from a squad car parked outside looked at me expectantly and with considerable relief. I let them in.

Having established me as the owner, they surveyed the aftermath of the battle. They were almost expres-sionless until they saw Miles's condition and I heard a sharp intake of breath from both of them. "Has anyone called an ambulance," the bearded one enquired and when I shook my head he went out to use the car radio. I introduced Lord Berridge to his companion as a friend and explained that it had been his phone call that had led to their timely arrival but he surprised us by admitting they had already been watching the shop on the instructions of Inspector Murdoch.

"He was concerned you might have some visitors and we were told not to make ourselves too obvious, so we parked quite a way off," the officer explained. "We saw these charmers arrive but from that distance couldn't be sure they weren't ordinary customers. There would have been rockets all round if we had burst in and arrested the wrong people. But when we saw the blind come down we reported in and were told to get over here. If Inspector Murdoch is on duty he'll probably be over too."

Berridge shrugged. "Well I did dial 999—so there should be another police car on its way."

The younger crook was taken out to the car while the bearded policeman helped Berridge and myself to lift the overturned bookcase and release the trapped man. He was more shocked than hurt; got to his feet stiffly and offered no resistance as he was led out. Meanwhile Berridge and I put the books back in some sort of rough order. No damage had been done and within a few moments the shop looked normal.

I was surveying the scene quite smugly when Murdoch arrived, looking quite pleased with himself. I looked over his shoulder to the street outside and saw several police cars and a small crowd beginning to gather. I felt an overpowering urge to tell them the fun was over and to go home but I desisted; excitement like this happened once in a lifetime in Ardley. I could expect reporters from the local paper in the next day or so.

Berridge made a short statement and I thanked him again for his assistance but taking the opportunity to remind him about the information I needed. He left, delighted with the experience—both books and battle. "We must do this more often," he said, quite wittily for him, as he closed the door behind him.

Murdoch was equally elated. "Just goes to demonstrate the value of co-operation," he crowed. "If we'd questioned Miles for a thousand years he wouldn't have talked. Catching him in the act is the best we could have hoped for . . . We might get a little more out of the others too although again I wouldn't expect too much."

"We don't need them any more. I *know* the name of the organiser . . . although proving it is another matter, at least to the satisfaction of the Director of Public Prosecutions."

"Lloyd?"

I nodded.

"He must be a millionaire or damn near. Why would he bother?"

"Precisely my reaction. Could be several things. For a start, when you total the sums involved it's not exactly peanuts. But my guess is that the book thefts are a front for something else. *What*, I'm not sure yet. But I paid him a visit last night . . . and guess what I found?"

He raised an eyebrow. "Presumably not any stolen books," he suggested, apparently thinking aloud. "I wouldn't care to hazard a guess. Depends on what you mean by 'found'? I trust you were there at his invitation?"

I smiled. "If you press me on that point I'll have to insist on my solicitor being here . . ."

He covered his face with a large hand. "Oh God, what have you let yourself in for?"

"I'll have to wait and see. You may have a decision to take in due course. Meanwhile, let's just say that Lloyd knows all about it. In fact we had a lengthy discussion and he's not prepared to take any action."

Murdoch raised his eyes to heaven but made no comment and I added rather irritably. "Do you want to hear what I found or don't you?"

He nodded. "Obviously none of this is admissible but it might at least colour my attitude towards you."

"That's all I can expect. In his private safe . . ." (I was conscious of his wince and pressed on determinedly) ". . . there were one or two things which might have been of interest to the fraud squad, if I could make head or tail of them, but what did stand out like a sore thumb was a sheaf of old invoices, mainly 19th century, from booksellers and auction houses of the period. What would he want with old book sale bills?"

"I don't know. Were the items listed of any significance?"

"No. But the headings are because its not difficult in most cases to remove the ink and add fresh information over the top, thus producing an apparently genuine bill of the right period. That in turn provides a stolen book

178

with a brand-new provenance."

He nodded. "It's an unprovable assumption but I take your point. Why *would* someone with no apparent interest in books have them in his safe?"

"The 64 dollar question . . . If Lloyd is using the books as a cover we should be trying to guess what that could be. I should mention that I also found a letter from someone in Marseilles, unfortunately in French, so I couldn't decipher it. Over dinner at Oldham Park he was talking about regular business trips to Europe, and France especially. But why was that letter in his private safe?"

Murdoch shrugged. "Could be something to do with a tie-up with the French underworld. Marseilles, as you know, is a key centre for smuggling of all sorts, drugs in particular."

I felt we were getting warm. Books seldom get very close attention from the customs people. The cheapest way to send books abroad, e.g., is to leave one end of the parcel open—to prove it is what it seems—thus making it eligible for reduced 'printed matter' rate. I pointed this out. "They are no more likely to be checked than an ordinary letter. Even books sent by ordinary parcel rate and marked clearly on the customs label outside are seldom checked. It didn't occur to me before because I was side-tracked by the value of the stolen books. Normally they would be sent insured and obviously, because of their value, attract rather more attention—and so a crook might hesitate about sending them that way . . ."

Murdoch seemed to get the drift. "You mean if the value of the book was considerably less than what they were trying to conceal, it's worth taking the risk?" I nodded and he concluded, "But what could you conceal in a book? Or rather what that would bear close scrutiny?"

"But it is feasible. If they just concentrated on the

179

more run-of-the-mill stuff no-one would look too closely at their phoney receipts, especially if they used photostats. So that brings us back to what they might be concealing . . . and how."

"Must be drugs," insisted Murdoch. "It offers the only profit margin that begins to justify the risk."

But how? We stared hopelessly at each other for a few moments and then suddenly a word from the Marseilles letter I had practically committed to memory flashed through my mind. I grabbed a French-English dictionary and looked up "relieur". The English word was bookbinder! I pulled a volume sumptuously bound in leather off the shelf and showed it to him. "Feel the thickness of that binding. You, like most people, think automatically of the modern cloth-bound books and of a hollow spine . . ." I put my finger down the spine of a different book to illustrate the point. "It's not unusual to have the covers built up and there are a number of possible permutations. You could have a false backstrip attached to the sewn area and concealed by a thick, decorated head-band . . . or pad out the leather on the spine itself and even insert a tube. You might have two boards instead of one board in the cover, leaving an 1/8th of an inch between. With a fairly common size of book, a demy 8vo, which is approximately $9'' \times 6''$, you can multiply that 1/8th thickness of powder by just over 100 square inches. It all adds up . . ."

He looked impressed. "Sounds very plausible. But we can't mount a nationwide check on book parcels leaving the country or coming in. Unless we can narrow it down considerably?"

"Why not? Forget about books leaving the country. If they wanted to re-export, Lloyd and his associates travel overseas frequently enough on legitimate business to transport the stuff without any hint of suspicion. Let's imagine that the books, probably relatively unimportant titles, are sent abroad to associates who arrange for an elaborate rebinding. The books are then returned full of heroin or cocaine. So let's concentrate on people who might be the recipients here. Lloyd is one likely bet. Another could be an honest executive, who may not even know what the books contain . . . could even be something innocuous like a set of Dickens or Walter Scott. Heyman is another possibility because his sudden death might have caught them on the hop. It takes at least a week for books to get here from Europe." I thought of adding Oldham Park to the list but stopped.

He nodded. "I don't see why not. We'll try to work something out with the customs people and the Post Office." He prepared to leave and commented for the first time on my swollen nose, "Miles's handiwork?"

It was simpler to nod and he added, "I should put some cold water on it pretty smartish—it's staring to swell up."

TWELVE

Caroline Berridge was never far from my thoughts and fortunately for my peace of mind I did not have to wait long to see her again. She paid her first visit to the shop on the pretext of surveying the scene of the 'battle', recounted it seemed with great enthusiasm by Lord Berridge. The excuse was plausible enough and Charlie accepted her curiosity without question, even confiding in her his own conviction that I had known or suspected there would be trouble in advance and had thoughtfully sent him home for his own safety. They regarded me with an admiration that was embarrassing, since it should have been obvious to Henry Berridge that I had been as surprised as him.

However, despite the innocent interpretation placed on Caroline's visit, I was inhibited by Charlie's presence, even when we went into the back room for tea. I longed to put my arms round her, yet when the door was finally closed we kept looking subconsciously in that direction, in case he should come in unexpectedly.

Caroline was more patient than me. "It's enough just to be with you," she said. "I've waited so long—another day or two hardly matters."

I kissed her, longing to do more, but controlling myself. "I can give Charlie a day off at any time," I pointed out.

She smiled. "You'd probably be overwhelmed with customers and I'd end up serving in the shop—which rather defeats the object! Could *you* take an afternoon off, tomorrow?" I nodded and she continued, "Come to me then. Henry will be out and it's the housekeeper's day off."

I accepted eagerly and she added, "While you're there I'll show you the accounts book that belonged to Henry's great-great-grandfather. I understand you'd like to see it . . ?"

My face flushed with embarrassment and I felt a surge of unreasonable anger at Henry's weakness. I had specifically asked him not to mention the request. Surprisingly she did not seem to notice anything strange in the way I had by-passed her so I did not complicate the issue with further explanation, merely nodding in a preoccupied way, as though I had more important things on my mind. Indeed the prospect of poring over an old record book when I might be doing something far more satisfying was almost depressing.

I knew relatively nothing about her and wanted o know everything. But Caroline was reticent—something else we had in common—even about generalities. She in turn wanted to know more about my background and since I was reluctant to elaborate either the conversation quickly petered out. We did at least see the funny side of our sudden apparent inability to communicate and finally settled for something more rewarding—another kiss. She touched my nose gently—the swelling had gone down but the bone had turned mauve—and then ran her fingers along my biceps appreciatively.

"Henry was absolutely bowled over by the way you handled those thugs—especially the leader," she said. "*Decisiveness* is what he admires; something he identifies with the officer class although frankly we always thought Billy has that sort of quality."

I'd forgotten about Lloyd and the fresh evidence and experienced a momentary qualm at the prospect of hurting her. Since I was confident now it was me she loved it seemed like kicking a man when he was down. But I had an obligation to tell her; there was always the possibility that he would in time make use of her or

183

the library in his search for riches or power—or whatever it was that motivated him.

I made her sit down before recounting what I had discovered and the search programme Murdoch intended to implement. As I had anticipated, she was shocked and upset although not as much as I had feared. There was an uncharacteristic edge to her voice when she responded. "I cried for Edward. He was a poor, wretched little man who got out of his depth but Billy is different. I feel I've been betrayed. We took him into our home, befriended him . . . not that it was any effort—he's a very likeable person . . . and now?" She broke off and looked at me sadly. I thought how vulnerable she looked and reached out for her but she held up a restraining hand. "Matt darling, are you absolutely certain?"

I nodded.

She smiled affectionately. "You wouldn't *lie* of course but you must admit you were just a tiny bit jealous of him?"

I shook my head. "Now that I *know* I'm not jealous of him any more," I said truthfully. "But I admire your loyalty; it does you credit. Just be on your guard from now on. Take another look at the concessions he has for catering and anything else."

She stood up and smiled sadly. "I'll do the things you suggest and I'll tell Henry, of course. He'll want to sever the connection at once but my conscience tells me not to rush into anything."

"Exactly. If the customs search comes to nothing Murdoch and I may have to eat our words. But somehow I don't think so."

We kissed and promised to meet at Oldham Park next day. Alone again I feared the next 24 hours would be the longest of my life.

Oldham Park's twelve acres were principally farmland

but the gardens surrounding the house conformed to the traditional image of the stately home. It had been closed to the public since my first meeting with the Berridges so I could ony imagine hordes of picnickers on the lawns and the flies and wasps swarming about overflowing litter-bins. I recalled sticky-fingered youngsters idly browsing through my stock of books, still clutching their ice lollies, and wondered how long it had taken Caroline and particularly Lord Berridge to accept the intrusion. They had no choice, admittedly, but that didn't make it any more acceptable.

There had been no message from Caroline so I left the shop just after lunch, telling Charlie where I was going but not bothering to contact Inspector Murdoch. Frankly, I wouldn't have known what to tell him and since he might have considered he was entitled to know I simply ducked the issue.

She answered the door herself and he first thing I noticed was that for a change she was wearing a dress, an elegant pale grey silk halter affair. Her shoes were a matching grey and she wore a flimsy white chiffon scarf at her neck. Her bare shoulders and arms were unblemished and held promise for the parts of her body as yet unseen. As soon as the door closed we kissed and she announced almost shyly that we had the entire house to ourselves. I wasn't sure whether it was shyness or a sudden formality when she said, "You've never seen the rest of the house. Why don't I give you the visitor's tour."

I did not wish to appear too single-minded but equally was not anxious to waste a precious hour or two studying family portraits and technical points of interest only to architects. I tossed the ball back. "Did you ask me here to practise your chat for the tourists?"

"The truth is you were fractionally early and I can't take you into the drawing-room yet—I haven't finished tidying up."

185

"What's wrong with the bedroom?"

She laughed. "Let me put *you* on the spot. Given a choice between making love to me—and browsing in the library, which would you choose?"

I pretended to give the matter some thought before deciding: "*You*, of course!"

"Thank you, darling—you're so gallant," she said with a sweet smile. "Then, if you wouldn't mind making do with your second choice first, you can take your time over the first later. First I must just clear up the mess."

I was amused at her illogicality. Who else but a woman would think about housework when about to entertain a lover? "Don't be ridiculous," I said gently. "As if I'd have eyes for anything but you." I took her arm and led her in the direction of the drawing-room, though conscious that she was literally dragging her heels. I could not believe she was really serious and laughingly pulled her into the drawing-room which, needless to say, was perfectly tidy apart from a pile of books in the centre of the room, lying amid layers of wrapping and corrugated paper, and string. The familiar lush green bindings indicated they had just arrived from France and I was a little surprised at the number of volumes. There were five large parcels, three still unopened, and a rapid calculation indicated that there must have been around 50 books. I would not have expected to have found more than a dozen books in the library that really needed rebinding so most of this consignment would come into the category of "cosmetic" work—which is an expensive business.

They were, however, beautiful to look at and I whistled in admiration. "Been on a spending spree?"

She smiled dutifully but her answer was serious. "Better than wasting it on a fur coat! I suppose I needn't have had them *all* done but the price is going up soon so we're saving money in the long run."

What she said made sense and I offered to help her finish unpacking.

She would not hear of it. "We should be here until midnight! Why do you think *I'm* so behind?"

I laughed. "We can try to be self-disciplined?"

She kissed me lightly on the lips. "This is not why you're here . . . Besides, I don't want to share you."

I warmed to her and returned the kiss. ". . . What books? When I'm with you everything else fades into the background."

She frowned slightly and her eyes bored into mine. "I believe you really mean that."

"Why should you doubt it?"

She sat down on the settee and pulled me down beside her. "From anyone else but you it would sound like a corny line in seduction. Language is a style of love-making that's new to me. Something else we have in common. We're both romantics. Dear Henry wouldn't know what I'm on about. He married a business partner, not a woman . . . someone who can look decorative about the place, impress his cronies and share the responsibilities. Oh, he appreciates me physically but its purely a biological response. He could never talk to me . . ."

I started to loosen the double bow of dress straps behind her back. "Talking only fulfils one function," I pointed out, conscious of an unsteadiness in my voice.

She removed my fumbling fingers and untied the straps herself. The silk fell away, revealing a flimsy, almost transparent bra through which her erect nipples strained. Her arms were suddenly around my neck and our lips met eagerly. My dreams were being realised at last and nothing else should have mattered at that moment, yet a sixth sense made me turn my head slightly and open my eyes. I was too late of course; in time to see but not prevent the blow aimed at my head. I had a split-second sense of revelation—and then a sharp pain and blackness.

I came round, aware of hands and feet being tied together behind my back. I was lying on my side on the carpet; directly in front of me Caroline was sitting on the settee. The person behind me grunted with the urgency or the effort of his task and even before he had finished I recognised the timbre of Lloyd's voice.

Caroline had one of the books recently arrived from France on her lap and she was very carefully using a razor blade to cut round the panel on the inside of the front cover. I watched in fascination as she lifted the board out completely and removed a flat, oblong plastic pouch. Opening a small flap at one end, she sniffed the contents, closed it again and put the pouch on top of several others on a side table. They obviously contained one of the illegal drugs—cocaine or heroin—in powder or crystal form.

When Lloyd moved round to join her he was stony-faced. Our eyes met but he looked away.

I felt almost a sense of disappointment in him. "With your brains, you didn't have to get mixed up in something as dirty as drugs," I remarked.

"Spare me the moralising," he replied. "People from my background can't afford morals."

"Don't give me that," I protested. "You can afford to do whatever you like. I can't believe you like getting kids hooked on drugs."

"I'm not selling to kids."

"But that's where the stuff ends up, down the line . . . with pushers making a beeline for decent youngsters—like your kid sister!"

He looked uncomfortable. "Those stories are exaggerated. They were pushing drugs when I was a kid; didn't influence me. Besides, I just bring the stuff in. It goes out straight away to a couple of distributors. We don't even repackage it."

I sneered. "You mean *you* only sell *pure* drugs. You're

not the ones who mix it with milk powder to quadruple the profits . . ."

"Knock it off, Coll!"

I stopped baiting him. "How did you get involved in the first place?"

"Some other time."

I tried a stab in the dark. "How's Pierre?"

He stopped in his tracks. "What d'you know about Pierre?"

"You've forgotten about the letter in your safe," I bluffed.

"Oh . . ." He was surprised, not doubting for a moment that I could read French. "Well, you don't want to worry yourself about Pierre—he can look after himself."

"I bet he can," I said, still guessing wildly. "And other people too!"

He laughed. "You've heard about him, have you?" I nodded and he continued as though proud of the association. "People talk of the French connection and I don't know which came first—the organisation or him. But he's Mr Big . . . more powerful than many government ministers . . . and certainly just as much beyond the law. First class organisation, private army, and ruthless as they come."

"You must make a good pair."

He took it as a compliment and nodded. "Pierre is very much a man of the time, a European. I needed him and he needs me."

"Who made the first approach?"

"I did. Got the idea when I discovered that Caroline had sent a couple of books to France for rebinding. I'd heard about a drug-smuggling ring and guessed they would always be interested in new ways of shipping the stuff over. So I made some enquiries. It wasn't really as straightforward as that. I heard later he only came in because of my business reputation in the City."

"So they handle everything on the Continent, and you take over at this end . . ?"

He nodded. "Pierre's people got a list of suitable craftsmen, picked a couple and then made them offers they couldn't refuse. They killed one bloke who didn't play ball."

"Charming people," I commented.

He grinned. "Strangely enough they are—the men at the top. No point in having partners you don't like."

"It was them behind Heyman's murder and the kidnapping? Or was that all part of your apprenticeship?"

"Why don't you figure it out," he replied indifferently.

I stared bitterly from the drugs to Caroline. "This is why you didn't want me in here? You have a flair for acting."

She smiled. "It wasn't *all* acting . . ."

She had practically finished removing the pouches and Lloyd informed her he was going to get his car. Incredibly, when he had gone I still clung forlornly to my shattered dream of the two of us. "You said it wasn't all acting—which part was which?"

She shrugged. "I had a job to do . . . we were playing for important stakes."

"You've told Lloyd . . . about us?"

"You make it sound underhanded. I don't see it that way. I love him. He's the first real man I ever knew."

The admission hurt. "What's your definition of a 'real man'?"

She smiled. "You came near to guessing when you compared our fathers—Billy's and mine. Using that yardstick, he has to be the complete opposite of my late father—*not* a gentleman, for a start. I admire people who go out and get, even take, what they want. Billy started from scratch. The fact that he's so attractive physically is just a bonus." She paused and looked at me mischievously. "If it's any consolation I find you just as attractive in one way—but with all due respect I don't see myself as the wife of a shopkeeper."

"Less lonely than being married to a gaolbird . . . prison is where Lloyd is heading. You too, by the look of things." She had finished removing the drugs and I was genuinely intrigued by the pile of damaged bindings. I asked what would happen to them.

"They were purpose-built. The binder flies over separately with his tools and just puts in a new inside board. It means merely that the leather dentelles will be slightly narrower."

"He comes over especially?"

She looked surprised at the question. "What's the cost of one air fare in relation to this little lot?"

"Money won't help you—in prison."

She shrugged gracefully. "We won't be around much longer. We planned for such a possibility *ages* ago."

"Wait until it actually comes to walking away and leaving all that money behind . . ."

"Money doesn't control our lives. That's another misapprehension of people like yourself."

I laughed. "If money wasn't that important why didn't Lloyd stop after making his first million? Why did he get mixed up in this dirty business? Don't tell me *you're* short of money?"

She laughed. "We have enough to be going on with. For Billy it was the excitement. Although he was glad to get out of the fight game he misses the excitement—the element of danger."

"So he thought up the robberies as a smoke-screen?" I said sarcastically. "It was entirely *his* idea and you were just an innocent bystander, caught up in circumstances beyond your control."

She regarded me with amusement. "That's a fair comment. I merely provided the motivation. Billy conceived the idea and developed it because he was

191

worried about my finances. It would never have *occurred* to me to do anything that might break the law."

"And Lord Berridge knows nothing about it?"

She sniffed contemptuously. "You must be joking."

Lloyd returned, looking as grim as before. "We'll take his car too," he said, addressing Caroline. "You drive behind till we get there; then we can use it to get to the station and leave it in the car park."

She nodded. "I've got everything packed and the note ready for Henry."

"Going somewhere?" I asked.

They ignored my question and Lloyd said to me "If I untie your legs you can walk to the car. If there's any fuss I'll carry you—unconscious. What's it going to be . . ?"

I didn't like the rasping tone of his uncharacteristic seriousness and sensed he was bracing himself for a distasteful job—getting rid of me. My anger was gradually replaced by apprehension.

"If you intend to kill me anyway why should I make it easy for you?"

"Then I'll do it here and save the bother," he said.

Caroline stood up and moved over to him. She lowered her voice although I still got the gist of her appeal for him not to 'do' it there. I began to lose hope. She obviously regarded me with no more concern than for a dog which had to be put down.

"Don't argue, children," I said, resigned. "I wouldn't want to come between lovers. I'll walk—on condition you'll tell me what's in store. The condemned man is entitled to one last wish."

Lloyd bent over and untied my ankles, making sure my wrists were still securely together. He helped me to my feet and muttered, almost swallowed, an apology for what was happening.

"No hard feelings," I said, "but don't keep me in suspense. Why not allow me the satisfaction of knowing

I wasn't a complete failure?"

A half-smile made him seem more like the 'old' Lloyd. "That you can have," he said, "but we knew it couldn't last for ever so we laid contingency plans . . . fresh identities abroad and rather a lot of money, even by our standards, in Swiss and Austrian banks. We'll just disappear and pop up on some golden beach as Mr & Mrs Smith."

"And what about me?"

"We haven't got time now," he said, pulling at my arm.

I looked at Caroline questioningly and she responded as though she felt I was entitled to know. "You must have guessed . . ."

I looked back to Lloyd but he avoided my eyes.

"The newspaper reports will say that Billy died in a car crash," interrupted Caroline. "People have always said he drives too fast. Then I'll walk off into the sunset with you—leaving a pathetic little note for Henry, imploring his forgiveness, and explaining that I was helpless against those dynamic qualities he admires himself."

The penny dropped. I shrugged. "Ah well, I always wanted to drive an Aston."

He snorted. "Well, since you know we may as well make the swop now. We won't bother with the clothes—there won't be much left after the fire." He removed the contents of my pockets and replaced them with bits and pieces from his own—an assortment of keys, small pocket diary, address-book and even a couple of elastic bands and paper clips. From his inside breast pocket he produced a pen and comb and a leather wallet, going through it carefully and even drawing my attention to £70 in bank notes before placing it inside my jacket. "Mustn't send you into the next world penniless," he said without a glimmer of a smile. I could see he was on edge, not relishing his actions. I wondered

193

if he had ever killed a man and doubted it.

I toyed momentarily with the notion of trying to fell him with a karate drop-kick but if I missed I would be unable to use my hands to offset the impact of hitting the ground. I might stand a better chance in the car when he was driving. With his concentration elsewhere I could try something—even with bound wrists.

Rather dejectedly I preceded him out, conscious of Caroline leaving an envelope on the table, the farewell message to Henry. I guessed that even now she was hedging her bets by putting the blame of me for 'seducing' her. If her plans with Lloyd did not work out and if she managed to avoid being linked with him the way was still open for a possible reconciliation with Berridge in the future. A not-too-bright Henry might easily be taken in again when asked to relate one "tragic" slip to the enormous contribution she had made to the success of Oldham Park.

Time was running out and I was conscious now of an element of desperation in my thought processes. My physical helplessness was especially frustrating; I could do nothing with my hands tied behind my back. Caroline opened the side door and looked both ways before signalling us to follow. A slight twinge of cramp in a back muscle was the hint I needed. I dropped to the ground with a cry of anguish and began to writhe in apparent pain. "Cramp!" I yelled. "For God's sake untie my arms."

Caroline shrank back uneasily but Lloyd was unmoved; staring down at me without emotion. "Come off it. I wasn't born yesterday."

I rolled on to my stomach and tried to move my arms within the limitations imposed by the rope. "Tie them to my sides if necessary," I pleaded, "but get them away from my back—it's agony."

He studied me for a second and then produced an automatic. "I was never one for causing unnecessary pain to dumb animals," he said, waving the gun in front of my face. "Sit up so that Caroline can untie your wrists."

He motioned her to get behind me and loosen the knots. My joints really were stiff and awkward, making it difficult for me to move them much, but he took no chances, instructing her to move away while I exercised them. "I don't have to remind you I can use this," he said. "Even if you move like greased lightning, from this distance I'm accurate to within a quarter of an inch."

When he considered the circulation in my arms was back to normal he told Caroline to retie the wrists, this time in front. I was forced to turn round again so that he had an unrestricted view of my back. I considered grabbing her and wheeling round with a human shield but realised he would kill me before I had turned 45 degrees.

But at least in front my arms were no longer completely useless. I followed Caroline into the gravel drive with Lloyd making up the rear and we walked to the Aston Martin parked nearby. Lloyd produced a gallon can of what I assumed to be petrol from the boot and set it down beside him. Then he handed my car keys to Caroline. "Fetch his car, Caro. The petrol can go in the back of that." He turned to me: "I know why you wanted your hands in front. If I'm driving, with you at the side, you could have a pretty good bash at throttling me . . . whereas if I let you drive you might do something rash and kill or injure the two of us. I seem to have this stupid kink about doing things the hard way . . . more of a challenge."

"It's a dilemma. I suggest you call the whole thing off."

He smiled sadly but did not have time to reply. We looked up at the sound of my Citroen approaching. Caroline got out and placed the can of petrol in the back. She seemed to have fewer qualms than Lloyd.

But then the three of us were stunned by a sudden shout or greeting from the distance and looked up to see Lord Berridge approaching. Our reactions were obviously different and I can only vouch for my own, which was one of extreme relief. I actually felt like hugging him. He was approaching across the lawns, the inevitable shotgun beneath a crooked arm, pointing downwards in the safety position. At a distance of 25 yards he had no reason to suppose anything was untoward—even at the rather obvious disappointment in Caroline's voice when she demanded to know what he was doing there . . .

"Bored with Anson's prattling," he announced, still having to shout at that distance. "Finally got on to pests. Nothing but theory so I walked out. Came back to change the gun."

I raised my bound wrists and waved them hopefully to attract his attention. He must have seen but possibly assumed his eyes were playing tricks because he did nothing. I wasn't all that surprised; it wasn't the sort of picture he might have expected to see. Luckily he came nearer and Caroline was forced to go towards him to cut off his view.

"Darling, thank God you've turned up. Something terrible has happened. We caught Matt prowling about in the library . . . then we found some of our books in his car. We were going down to the police station when you arrived."

Totally confused, Berridge slowed to a halt, looking from them to me. "You've got the wrong end of the stick, old girl. Matt's not a thief, any more than I am. Must have jumped to conclusions."

I waved my hands again and he was even more confused. "Why is he tied up?" he demanded of Caroline.

She had reached him and was clinging to his arm

pathetically. "It was terrible, darling. We thought he'd have an explanation—but then he suddenly went berserk."

"She's lying," I called out. "Look what Lloyd has concealed in his right hand. Since when have you invited him to Oldham Park for target practice?"

Berridge looked at him suspiciously. "What d'you say to that?"

Lloyd raised the automatic and pointed it at Lord Berridge. "No time for explanations now, Henry. We've got to get him away from here. He's dangerous—so you stay out of it."

I interrupted. "They've made fools of us all, Henry. You've caught them running off together. They were going to kill me first but now it looks as though you'll have to join me."

Berridge started to straighten his shotgun ominously but Caroline clung to his arm. "Don't believe him, darling—he's lying." He said nothing but his eyes continued to glitter dangerously and I saw Lloyd's trigger finger begin to tighten in anticipation. I swung both fists against his extended arms, jerking them up so that the bullet fired skywards. Meanwhile Berridge reacted instinctively. With one arm he shook Caroline free and with the other steadied the gun and fired, without seeming to take aim. The discharge caught Lloyd in the stomach and the impact at less than a dozen yards knocked him off his feet.

He fell behind me so that I could have reached him in three or four strides. But I was stopped in my tracks by Caroline's piercing scream and stood transfixed as she rushed towards us. She bundled past me to kneel at Lloyd's side. She cradled his head in her lap, oblivious of the blood that vomited in small jets from a gaping wound. Almost immediately the front of her beautiful dress was dyed crimson—a sight horrific enough to send most women, and probably most men, into a faint; but

197

her eyes never left his face. She seemed totally unaware of the wet mess that continued to saturate her dress. It was obvious to me that Lloyd was losing too much blood to survive the wound and there was no way to stop it outside a hospital surgery.

Berridge was in shock—rooted to the spot from which he had fired—and even when I shouted at him to ring for an ambulance he did not respond. I hesitated between going myself or trying to see what I could do for Lloyd before he died. At that moment he opened his eyes and saw me. "There's a phone in my car," he said, almost as though he was reading my thoughts, "but don't bother. I won't last that long."

Caroline protested tearfully but I could see he was right. His pupils began to blur and he seemed to lose the ability to focus. It took an obvious effort of will for him to concentrate on the anxious face so close to his; then he smiled at her with affection.

"Sorry, my love," he said gently, as though addressing a favourite child. "I couldn't follow through this time, when it really mattered."

She kissed his face tenderly and I saw the tears rolling down her cheeks. I had seen her cry before and knew now how much of an act it had been. This was the real thing—a grief that was cutting through her like a knife through butter. Her beautiful face was twisted in anguish and she struggled to hold back the sobs so that he would not realise why she cried. I was moved. My pangs of jealousy earlier seemed suddenly superficial and unworthy in the face of this reciprocated love.

He moved his gaze to encompass me and I knelt on the other side of Caroline.

". . . Matt . . . Try to leave Caroline out of it. . . . It was me . . . I planned everything."

His eyes began to glaze; he stopped and rested and I doubted whether he would speak again. He lay with his eyes closed, his breathing shallow.

Misunderstanding, Caroline relaxed. "That's it, my darling. You rest . . . the ambulance is coming."

I was suddenly aware of Berridge walking past us to the Aston Martin, using the car radio to summon an ambulance and the police. When he returned Lloyd's face was grey. The bleeding seemed to be easing off but I suspected only because there was little left. He was lying in a huge reddish-brown pool and the entire front of Caroline's dress was drenched. Then surprisingly he opened his eyes once and they were clear. They rested on Caroline's face and he smiled. He was at rest. Then the smile slowly faded and he died.

THIRTEEN

For 24 hours I felt numb, as though I was under sedation. The successful outcome of the investigation already seemed an anti-climax. Something was missing; difficult to define. A sense of loss . . . a restlessness . . . the outcome perhaps of discovering a new world, with the fascinating people who inhabit it, and the inevitable reluctance to return to the old one. Lloyd and Heyman, whom I liked and respected in different ways, were dead, and Caroline might just as well have been.

Even the shop, which had once been the centre of my world, seemed less important although I was rational enough to realise that some of the enthusiasm would eventually come back. And when I contacted Laura to tell her the news the call was more an obligation than a pleasure. She was just an old friend; there was no spark. I hoped, for both our sakes, it might be rekindled—but even that response was mechanical and without any real warmth. Fortunately she had no cause to doubt my excuses about being 'tied' to Ardley for the next few weeks to 'catch up' with the backlog of work that had accrued in my absences. I promised to contact her when she might come down for a weekend, hinting there was little time for relaxation in the immediate future. Yet Laura was an independent girl and her "don't call me—I'll call you" was phrased in a friendly enough manner.

At the initial court hearing—moved nearly 50 miles away because the Berridges were known to the local magistrates—the police asked for remands in custody to enable further enquiries to be made. Lord Berridge entered a plea of 'not guilty' to murder and Caroline 'not guilty' to one charge of stealing certain specified books although Murdoch told the magistrates that other charges would be preferred at a later date. Berridge stared straight ahead. He recognised no-one, clearly wanted no sympathy and seemed to regard the case as a matter strictly between him and the court. Caroline was as poised as ever yet looked strangely vulnerable. Her face kept turning in my direction and I realised the first time our eyes met that even the traumatic discovery of her relationship with Lloyd had not got her out of my system. I managed to sneak a longer look when her attention was taken by the magistrates or counsel for the Crown. She seemed tired and under considerable strain.

The hearing lasted barely ten minutes. No evidence was taken. Despite the seriousness of the charge against Lord Berridge bail was granted without hesitation; although, admittedly, the prosecution did not press the matter—there had even been some suggestion, according to Murdoch, that the charge might be reduced to one of manslaighter. Ironically Berridge looked the part; that imperious expression, the upturned profile, seemed to fit the role in which he had been cast—as an honourable young Englishman betrayed by an unscrupulous wife. And when the bench was told that a forged passport had been found in Caroline's possession the tone and expression of Geoffrey Davidson, the chairman, made it apparent that he fully accepted police fears that she might try to leave the country and had no hesitation in refusing her application. I was disturbed by such Victorian attitudes and wondered if it would influence my evidence when the trial started.

Murdoch told me later that for 48 hours Caroline had been totally apathetic, refusing to talk to anyone—but that after the second visit of her solicitor she had started to show a little interest in her defence. Her case would be that she had been infatuated with Lloyd; that she had no influence on his actions; that most of the time she had been unaware of what was happening and that her own eventual involvement had been quite insignificant. When Murdoch asked for my impressions I hesitated. Infatuated she might have been—her subsequent grief had been no act—but she undoubtedly had known what she was doing. She had admitted as much before the shooting. Whether or not it was merely to protect Lloyd she had also been a willing enough participant in the plan not only to kill me but to dispose of my body. She was certainly less squeamish than Lloyd. Yet I could not bring myself to 'gang up' on her. Caroline's world was in ruins; there was little point in turning the screw. I gave a non-committal reply and changed the subject. I wanted to know, for example, if the police now considered the case closed.

He squinted so that the shaggy brows practically covered his eyes. "It's not for me to say but you've probably got a better feel for the case than I have. If you're satisfied that Lloyd provided the brains and the organisation, and Miles and his cronies the muscle and break-in expertise, I don't see what else we can do."

I had to agree but pointed out that very few of the really valuable books had been traced.

"Recovering stolen property is something of a lottery," said Murdoch. "Largely a matter of luck. It's faintly possible we might get something from one of the villains but they probably didn't know where the books went—theirs not to reason why and all that."

Next day I had a telephone call from Maurice Rawlinson, Caroline's solicitor and senior partner in the Exeter firm of Rawlinson, Manning and Hopes. He asked if I could spare the time to see him phrased so politely that I was immediately suspicious of his motives—still more, when he admitted his reluctance to come to Ardley. "While I'm not doing anything

202

underhand, I have to be careful that my actions are not misconstrued as interference with witnesses," he explained.

My reaction at the time was dominated by thoughts of Caroline. Had she sent him? And if so—why? We agreed to meet the same evening at a 17th century inn, the Charles II, just off the B3177 at Ottery St Mary, which was conveniently situated about halfway between us.

Rawlinson was a well-groomed, heavily built man in his late forties. There was an air of confidence about him that seemed to label him as a lawyer. His background was difficult to identify; the voice had absolutely no accent at all, as though he had worked on it. He may have been a product of one of the red-brick universities but wherever, I guessed he had come down with a First and had maintained that sort of standard throughout his legal career. He had the presence I would have expected of someone associated with Caroline and was probably more suited to the case in hand than the firm of family lawyers who represented Lord Berridge—although the counsel they had briefed was one of the country's foremost QCs.

Rawlinson bought us both pints of the local brew and then came straight to the point. "I should explain," he began, "that Lady Berridge was against me seeing you. To be perfectly frank, it's been a tremendous effort to persuade her to offer any defence at all. She seems to feel she *ought* to be punished—and that anything said in her defence smacks of legal chicanery."

"Then why doesn't she plead guilty?" I asked.

"Our legal system fortunately recognises the fact that defendants are not necessarily the people who know best. I happen to believe she is innocent but at the moment she wants to take the blame for everything—including the shooting."

"The shooting?"

"That too. At least, she says she feels responsible. Naturally, as an eye-witness she will support the self-defence plea, as indeed you presumably will. But she insists on bringing up the matter of provocation, which is really irrelevant in a case of self-defence."

"What do you mean?" I asked.

"Well, you must remember . . . Lloyd taunting her husband about his inadequacy as a lover."

It was news to me but I let it go. "What do you want me to say then?" I asked pointedly.

He flushed. "There's no need to be cynical, Mr Coll. I'm sure all we both want is for the truth to emerge."

"The truth *will* emerge. Why do we have to rehearse it?"

He smiled. "I shouldn't have come. I'm skating on thin ice as it is—but I didn't want to stand by while my client simply threw in the towel . . . to invite a prison sentence in order to punish herself—not for this crime—but for slipping below her own very high moral standards."

High moral standards? That was a laugh. I was torn between the irony of Rawlinson's falling into the same trap as me and fear that there might be an element of truth in what he said and that Caroline really wanted to go to prison. My conscience rebelled at the prospect. "You may as well finish what you were saying," I conceded.

Rawlinson ordered another round of drinks. "Since counsel is not allowed to lead a witness it's quite possible that certain vital information might never be disclosed if it slips a witness's mind. Before Lloyd died did he say anything to you?"

I remembered the scene vividly. "Not much, but that *he* planned the robberies and that she wasn't involved."

He sighed with relief. "I couldn't rely on getting that out of my client. I think perhaps now I can see some light at the end of the tunnel."

I was intrigued. "What does she say about her role in the events leading up to the shooting?"

He shrugged. "Only the truth . . . that is, everything she can remember. Parts of her memory are complete blanks but she recalls odd sequences, such as tying you up or untying you, as Lloyd instructed. We hope to show that she was frightened for her safety or even her life . . ."

"Why should she be frightened of the man with whom she was apparently infatuated?"

"Because he was behaving irrationally. And he had a gun."

"Does she remember how Lloyd happened to overpower me?" This was the 64 dollar question. I had not yet decided how I would deal with that myself or rather how much I would reveal. In my statement to the police I had carefully skated over certain parts of my story. He would have seen a copy of that statement and shown it to his client.

Rawlinson's brow was furrowed. "I'm not sure. I seem to remember she was showing you an old record book in the library when Lloyd crept up from behind and then hit you over the head with the butt of a gun. It seems he'd been following you, waiting for a chance to shut you up once and for all."

I wondered whether it really mattered. If I announced to the world that we were on the point of making love when—with her prior knowledge—Lloyd attacked me her credibility would be destroyed. Things were already stacked against her and I doubted whether I could put the boot in too.

Rawlinson was more relaxed. "Bearing in mind what Lloyd told you at the end, you have no evidence that Lady Berridge was involved in the thefts—apart, of course, from what she did under duress."

I considered, ". . . apart from that, no evidence."

He smiled gratefully and stood up. "I've got a pile of

paperwork to catch up with." We shook hands and went our separate ways.

Back at Ardley I reread Heyman's letter for the umpteenth time. The personal bits to which Murdoch had referred were somewhat rambling but there was an enlightening passage about Caroline although he had not named her. Careful as he was to avoid implicating the woman with whom he was infatuated, Heyman's odd pieces of information completed the jigsaw and I finally realised the true sequence of events.

I knew now it had been Caroline who approached the librarian—not the other way round although, short of asking her, there was no way I would ever discover the tack she had used. The plan must still have been in its infancy when she inveigled Lloyd's help. He had organised the operation on a nationwide basis, blackmailing Heyman and using professional thieves—before changing course to concentrate on smuggling.

The trial was front page news. Although he had been allowed to stay at Oldham Park Berridge had aged dramatically from the strain and the humiliation of public exposure. He was as poker-faced as ever but there were lines that I had never noticed before. In contrast Caroline looked even more beautiful despite her spell in prison. She was already something of a celebrity and I had received a request from the Daily Chronicle to use my 'influence' to persuade her to sell them her story. I had refused but knew they would persist and eventually win her over—for a five-figure sum.

I was called to give evidence on the second day. In the opening minutes, as I took the oath and went through the motions of identifying myself and my position, I was conscious only of Caroline's penetrating stare. When finally I met her eyes she smiled, almost shyly. I felt nothing; seeing a mask of beauty but little humanity beneath. John Austin, QC for the Crown, took me through the preliminary questions, establishing my role in the investigation, before finally reaching the nub of the matter.

"On the day of Mr Lloyd's death did you go to Oldham Park?"

"I did."

"And what was the purpose of that visit?"

I looked at Caroline and she smiled reassuringly. I thought of Heyman, then of Loyd. And when she saw my expression the smile froze. I continued to stare at her as I told my story—filling in the blanks. It was time for the reckoning.